Desert Gold

Other Avalon Books by S. R. Hawley

DEADLY SECRETS

DESERT GOLD

S. R. HAWLEY

AVALON BOOKS
THOMAS BOUREGY AND COMPANY, INC.
401 LAFAYETTE STREET
NEW YORK, NEW YORK 10003

PRINTED IN THE UNITED STATES OF AMERICA
ON ACID-FREE PAPER
BY HADDON CRAFTSMEN, SCRANTON, PENNSYLVANIA

To Mike Lawrence—
who never pushed me for the rent

Chapter One

*A*llison Ames paused for a moment to catch her breath and watched hopelessly as Dr. Terry Braun marched vigorously up the side of the sand dune, widening the gap between them.

As though sensing Allison's growing desperation, Braun stopped in midstride and turned to face his hiking companion. His khaki shirt was splotched with sweat. "Not much farther," he called with an encouraging tone. "We'll take a rest at the top."

Allison took a deep breath and wiped her forehead. She wanted to shout a reply but lacked the strength. Her body seemed to simmer in the heat. A blazing summer sun beat mercilessly upon the barren Arizona landscape. She wiped moist palms against her thighs and plunged up the loose, flowing sand of the dune.

She remembered Terry Braun's helpful if somewhat persistent personality from dealings the two had previously shared. Allison's career as a free-lance writer often led her to unusual people. Some were eccentric, like the worm rancher in Washington, and others were chilling, like the convicted killer in California, but

Terry Braun, professor of geology at Arizona State University, was by far the most goal-oriented man she had ever met. He probably didn't realize that he had set such a tiring pace up the dune.

Sand ran over her boots as they sank into the mountain of sand. She leaned into the hill and tried to forget her misery. The fabric straps of her two nearly full canteens bit into the soft flesh of her neck, and the camera bag she had slung over her shoulder swung in wild arcs, bouncing off her hips. Perspiration trickled across her cheeks from under the brim of the brown fedora she wore. A hot spot on the bottom of her left big toe portended a blister and served to increase her misery.

The months that had passed since their last meeting had laid a haze to her memory of the friendly, easygoing geology professor. She had been working on a piece about prehistoric Arizona at the time, and the two had scoured the high country near Flagstaff for fossils. It had seemed to Allison that he had done much more than was necessary to provide background for the article.

She had wondered at the time whether he had simply been expressing pride in his profession or whether his intentions had involved more personal motives. He certainly had seemed interested in her daily doings.

Her research had ended, though, and the two had not been in contact since.

She plodded heavily through the sand. Ahead of her, Terry continued to move steadily up the side of the dune. There was no doubt but that he was as fit as an athlete.

The fossil article had brought Allison a tidy sum, and

she had gradually forgotten about Terry. When she had realized, however, that she needed an expert to help her complete an article for *Rock Hound* magazine, she had been eager to give him a call.

Terry continued to move steadily up the side of the dune. From her position halfway up its side, Allison surveyed the surrounding desert. The ground shimmered in the heat.

She ran a finger under the edge of her canteen straps. Her tongue was dry, and her lips were caked with dried perspiration and salt.

She was safe, she knew, as long as she felt her thirst and continued to perspire. Travelers in the desert faced danger when they stopped sweating and no longer realized their need for water.

Terry rounded the summit of the dune. He turned to Allison and called. "It's a great view from here. You'll get a good bird's-eye vantage point to describe the location."

She smiled and waved. By this time she wasn't so much concerned with the view as with settling down for a long drink from her canteen. She continued to climb the dune. The distance to the top closed with agonizing slowness.

Noticing Allison's effort, Terry shouted, "I didn't mean to speed ahead." He glanced at the scenery and again reported on the excellent view.

She assumed that his repeated exclamations regarding the landscape were his way of apologizing for the arduous hike, and she couldn't help but smile to herself. "All I want to see is a canteen of water," she said as she neared the crest of the dune.

"It's ready and waiting," he replied, displaying a round, blanket-covered canteen. "You get the first drink," he said with a smile, unscrewing the cap.

Bathed in perspiration and breathing heavily, Allison topped the crest and accepted Terry's proffered canteen. She slouched to the ground to rest, but she was wearing shorts, and the scorching sand burned her exposed skin. She yelped with pain and jumped to her feet.

"Watch out, that sand is hot," Terry said, helping her up. His grip was strong on her elbow.

"I've got to be more careful," Allison commented. She rubbed the sand from her thighs, then drank thirstily from the canteen.

Though the water was warm, she swallowed it happily. It was tinged with the plastic taste of the canteen liner, but she hardly noticed.

"Better take it easy," he said. "Too much of that in this heat, and you'll be curled up, sick as a dog, under the shade of the nearest creosote bush."

Allison knew his advice was well-founded. Too much water in the condition she was in, and she ran the risk of stomach cramps and nausea. She lowered the canteen. "I needed that," she said with a grateful smile.

He returned her smile. "May I?" he asked, reaching for the canteen.

"Oh, I'm sorry," she said with a self-conscious laugh. She had forgotten about her own canteen slung around her neck.

Terry swallowed some of the water. Allison noticed that he hadn't wiped the lip of the canteen. It gave her a curiously comfortable feeling.

"It's not easy getting old," he said when he was finished. "There was a time when I could have made that climb without even raising a sweat. But now. . . ." He tugged at his sweat-stained shirt and shrugged. "I'm not as young as I once was."

"You're not an old man yet. You can't be more than twenty-five."

"I'll take that as a compliment," he said. "Actually, I'll soon be thirty." He smiled at Allison. "You're twenty-four, aren't you?"

She was pleasantly surprised that he would remember such a seemingly insignificant detail from their previous dealings. "I've had a birthday since then," she said. "I'm twenty-five."

"You let me miss your birthday?" he asked teasingly. "I probably would have taken you out."

"I accept rain checks."

"Glad to hear it," he said, still grinning. "Now that you're reaching Social Security age, have you discovered any gray hairs?"

"I haven't been searching," she replied with mock indignance. A gentle breeze wound its way through her simply styled blond hair. "But I think a man of your advanced years would have a better chance of finding them than I would."

Terry considered her statement. "You're right." He reached over and ran his fingers through a few strands of her hair. "Give me a few minutes sometime, and I'll see if I can find any."

"I meant in your own head." She laughed, playfully slapping his hand down. A thrill tingled through her body. There could be no doubt now that professional concerns weren't the only reason Terry had agreed to accompany her into the desert. "Anyway, we're not supposed to be out here hunting for gray hairs, remember?"

He snapped his fingers. "Turquoise!" he exclaimed, pretending that he had forgotten the reason for the trip.

"Yes, turquoise," she repeated with a grin. She unstrapped her canteen and drank some more. "I hope we're almost there."

"As a matter of fact, we're here." Terry gestured in a wide arc with his arm. He scanned the desert beyond the dune. "We'll make our way up that wash." He pointed to a draw that cut a narrow gorge between two gravel-strewn hills. The hillsides shimmered in the heat. Creosote and barrel cactus sprouted here and there from the scorched earth. The mouth of a wash was obscured by a jutting promontory of red rock.

Allison followed his gaze. "You think that looks promising?"

"I found some turquoise there the last time I was here. I'm sure we'll find some more this time." He turned his attention from the wash and looked at her. "Tell me if I'm going too fast."

Allison thought she detected a trace of guilt in his voice. "I think I'll be able to keep up with you going downhill," she said. The short pause and the water had refreshed her.

"I'll tell you what," he offered. "I'll move off ahead of you, travel up that wash, and try to locate a turquoise bed. Then I'll lead you to the general area, and you can put your research to the test. We'll see if you can locate the turquoise on your own."

Allison agreed to the idea, and they set off down the dune. Terry quickly outdistanced her.

When he reached the bottom, he stomped onto the gravel of the surrounding desert, shaking sand from his socks and boots. He turned and faced Allison, nearing the end of her descent. "I'm going to move on," he said, pointing vaguely toward the wash. "I won't be far."

"That's fine," she responded. She made the base of the dune and stopped for a moment to enjoy a quick sip from her canteen. She was amazed that he was able to maintain such a vigorous pace. He was, she could tell, in excellent physical condition.

She quickly recapped her canteen and set off along the path that Terry had chosen. When she made her way around the jutting edge of the red-rock promontory, she discovered that the wash that Terry had indicated was, in reality, two washes. They forked around a fall of boulders and snaked their way through the rugged, rock-strewn terrain.

She quickly glanced to the sandy ground, searching for Terry's footsteps as a clue to which direction she should travel, but found no indication of his passing.

She stood momentarily at the fork, trying to decide which way to turn, when she suddenly heard Terry calling her name.

"Allison, Allison!"

She snapped her head in the direction of his voice and froze. Had he fallen and hurt himself?

"Allison," he called again, "come here quickly."

There was an urgency in his tone that she could not deny. She ran up the side of the draw but saw nothing except barren, broken desert terrain.

"Come on, come on," he shouted.

The tone of his voice compelled her to hurry. She scrambled up the side of the draw, her canteens and camera swinging wildly, her feet skittering over the loose gravel. "Where are you?" she called.

"Down here," he shouted. "There's a man here. Quick, he needs help."

She listened to Terry and hurried in the direction of his voice.

"He's mumbling something in Spanish," he shouted. "Come on, come on, hurry."

She dodged through a stand of cholla cactus. She noticed a shoe lying on the hot gravel of the desert floor.

"Come on!"

Suddenly, Terry popped over the crest of the hill that separated the two washes. He was waving his arms frantically. "Hurry up," he shouted. "You know Spanish, right?"

She didn't answer. She devoted her energy to running. She noticed a shirt draped in a tangled heap on the branches of a creosote bush.

Terry's head disappeared as he ducked down the side of the draw. Allison rushed over the crest of the hill and immediately spotted him, on his knees, hovering over the still form of a man wearing only a pair of filthy trousers. She ran down to them.

Terry glanced up from the man. "I heard him moaning," he said.

Allison studied the man lying on his back on the hot earth. He was old, and his ribs bulged through the skin of his chest.

A thin sound emanated from somewhere deep in his throat.

She gazed with horror at the man's mouth. His lips were dry and cracked, and his tongue was swollen so that it protruded slightly between his teeth.

Terry poured a trickle of water from his canteen into the palm of his hand and let it drip into the man's mouth. "He's dying of thirst," he said.

The old man's jaw worked slowly as the water dripped into his open mouth. His throat lurched as he tried to swallow.

"There's no telling how long he's been out here," Terry said.

The man mumbled something.

"Can you make out what he's saying?" Terry asked.

Allison leaned forward and laid her ear close to the man's mouth. His voice was faint and his words badly slurred, but Allison thought she heard him mention a name. "Rosa," he said.

She hovered there, waiting for him to continue. "My wife," he said in Spanish. "Tell my wife." Then again, the name, "Rosa."

Allison leaned back as Terry allowed more water to drip down the old man's throat. They watched silently as he forced himself to swallow. "He's in a bad way," Terry told her.

Suddenly the old man's eyes widened, as though he had understood what Terry had said. He reached up and grabbed Terry's shirt. His hands shook as they clung to the sweat-soaked fabric.

"The gold," he hissed in Spanish. "It is mine."

Terry glanced at Allison. "What's he saying?"

She quickly translated.

"Gold? What the devil?"

The old man continued to cling to Terry's shirt. "Murder," he said. "Tell my wife I love her."

Allison quickly interpreted what the old man was saying. Suddenly he burst into speech again, a long, rambling discourse that Allison could not understand.

"He's hallucinating," Terry explained. He set his canteen down at his feet and disengaged the old man's hands from his shirt. "It's all right," he said in a soothing tone.

Allison cradled the man's head in her hands.

All the strength seemed to leave the old man. Terry allowed some more water to trickle down his throat.

For the first time Allison was able to get a good look at the helpless victim of the desert heat. His skin was red, and hot to her touch, and his bare feet were covered with cuts and abrasions.

Suddenly he spoke again. ". . . followed me." His voice was a ragged whisper, and his words nearly impossible to understand. In rapid translation Allison relayed to Terry everything he said to her.

The old man continued to speak. "Murdered me."

"Who?" Terry asked. "Ask him who."

"*¿Quién?*" Allison asked in a soft tone.

The old man struggled to speak. "P . . . P . . . P," he stuttered, laboring with heavy breath, but he could not find the strength to form the name. He closed his eyes; his chest heaved.

"Nogales," he said. "Tell Rosa I love her."

"I'll tell her," Allison responded.

"*Bien,*" the old man said. "Good."

He stopped speaking. His eyes were closed and his breathing shallow and rapid.

Terry shook his head. "He doesn't have much time. Look." He lifted one of the man's hands. The fingers were raw and bloody from clawing at the ground. "I found a man once in the Grand Canyon who was dying of thirst. He was scratching at the earth, eating dirt, and mumbling all sorts of incoherent thoughts." He was silent for a moment, staring at the old man. "He was in better shape than this guy, but he was dead inside of fifteen minutes."

"What are we going to do?" she asked.

He was silent for several seconds as he allowed a small amount of water to trickle down the man's throat. "Look at this," he said at last, again lifting the man's hand. "The cuts are barely bleeding."

She eyed the man's injuries. It was true. The blood oozed from the cuts slowly, like glue.

"He's been without water for so long that his blood has thickened. I don't think there's much we can do for him."

Though Allison realized that he was probably right, Terry's comments somehow angered her. "We can't just ignore him," she said. "We have to do something."

Before Terry could respond, the old man opened his eyes. "P . . . P. . . ." His breath sputtered weakly. "P . . ." he uttered one last time. His head rolled heavily to the side.

Terry tilted his ear to the old man's chest and listened for several seconds. He arose and shook his head. "He's dead," he said.

Allison stared helplessly at the old man's silent form.

"There was nothing we could do," Terry was saying.

"I know." She had covered tragedy and death in her wanderings as a writer, but never had she witnessed it this closely, this horribly, or been this involved.

"Really," Terry said, seeming to sense her reluctance to accept the fact. "He'd been too long without water."

They remained silent for several minutes. Finally Allison asked, "What do we do now?"

"We hike out. And notify the authorities."

As they stood to leave, Allison glanced down at the man's body. "I feel strange," she said, "just leaving him here."

"We can't carry him out," Terry told her. He glanced at the terrain around him. "The desert is a cruel place. The rules of civilized society don't apply out here. When we get to Kingman, we'll notify the police, and they'll send someone to pick him up."

Allison continued to stare at the body, unwilling to leave.

"Let's go," Terry said softly. He placed a hand on her shoulder and turned her away from the grim sight.

They hiked through the desert toward Terry's Jeep in silence. At last Allison spoke. "What do you think he was talking about?" she asked. "About the gold, I mean."

Terry shook his head. "No idea," he said, kicking a stone with his boot. "This is gold country, though. The desert is pocked with old mines."

"Do you think he was searching for one?" She stopped for a moment to drink from her canteen.

He mulled her proposition. "If he was, he was looking in the wrong place. All the gold to be found in these parts was mined out long ago. Even when the stuff was selling for eight hundred an ounce, no one was starting new mines around here. This area is spent."

"What do you think he was talking about, then?" Though she didn't want to mention it, the old man's talk of murder weighed heavily on her mind.

Terry shrugged as Allison screwed the top back onto her canteen. "It's probably all a bunch of nothing. He was crazy from heat and thirst and most likely hallucinating. I doubt whether even he knew what he was saying."

They continued hiking. "But," Allison countered, "he seemed lucid enough to recall his wife's name and where she lived." In the back of her mind, she pictured the old man's widow learning of her husband's death. The thought filled her with sadness.

"There's no telling what thoughts were racing through his mind," Terry said. He walked a while longer. "But that talk about murder and gold. . . ." He shook his head and shrugged. "Hallucinations."

They continued to hike from the desert. Allison was relieved that at least Terry had slowed his pace. Still, the heat of the day was taking its toll on her, and they stopped for a short rest.

She opened her canteen to drink as Terry examined some rocks at his feet. Turning back to survey the path they had just traversed, she thought she noticed a movement, something on the rim of a wash, too far away to be clearly seen. "What's that?" she asked.

Terry glanced up. "What's what?"

"That," Allison said, pointing at the distant figure just as it dipped from view into a wash.

"I don't see anything," Terry said. "Must have been a mirage or something."

"I'm sure I saw something."

"Maybe a coyote."

The thought of a wild animal prowling near the body of the dead man sent a shiver up Allison's spine.

She was hot, tired, and depressed. "I just want to get out of here and call the police," she said. She pictured the scavenging coyote and shuddered.

"All right." Terry placed a gentle hand on her shoulder. "We have a couple of miles yet to the Jeep."

Chapter Two

*A*llison's phone jangled in the living room. She sat at her desk in the spare room she used as an office and listened to it ring. The computer monitor before her displayed a blank screen.

The ringing intruded on her thoughts. She considered ignoring it. She was afraid that if she allowed an interruption, she would never get started on her new article. The ringing persisted, however, daring her not to answer. Finally she relented.

She crossed the soft carpet of her living room and plopped onto the sofa with a sigh of resignation before lifting the receiver. Terry's voice met her ear.

"Allison," he said, "I was wondering if you had a few minutes to talk."

Allison considered the blank screen waiting for her in her office. She knew that the article she was working on would never get finished if she procrastinated, but she had been wanting to speak with Terry about the events of the previous day. "I think I could make some time," she said lightly.

Terry's voice on the other end sounded loud and

cheerful. "Good. I was wondering if you'd heard any word on the old man."

"I called Kingman this morning. They still had no ID on him."

The line was silent for a moment. "It's rough," Terry said with feeling. "To go like that, I mean."

Allison sat quietly for a minute. She and Terry had hiked back to his Jeep on the powerline road and raced back to Kingman as quickly as possible to report the incident in the desert. The sheriff's department had dispatched a helicopter to recover the body while the pair had filled out the necessary reports. After several hours in the police station, they had been permitted to return to their homes in Mesa, a four-hour drive away.

"The police are running down leads in Nogales," Allison said. "They're trying to find his wife."

Terry grunted. "Good luck. There must be over a thousand Rosas in that city."

"Maybe," Allison said. "But they say one of his teeth had a gold cap and that the cap was inscribed with the initials of the dentist who did the work. They hope to trace the dentist and locate dental records that will yield a positive identification."

Terry sounded incredulous. "You mean, the dentist signed his work?"

Having written an article about the diamond business, in which she had learned that diamond cutters often inscribe a nearly imperceptible personal mark on the diamonds they fashion, Allison had not been overly surprised to learn from the Kingman police that the same practice was customary among dentists. It was, in fact, a great aid to police departments, which were often forced to make identifications based solely on the dental records of anonymous victims.

She explained the circumstances to Terry, who listened quietly.

"So there's a good chance that the old man will be identified," he concluded.

"It seems so."

The line was silent for a moment. Finally Terry spoke. "I was sorry you had to see that."

"I've had better days. It's just so awful when you think about it. That poor old man wandering around in that terrible heat. If it weren't for that gold cap, chances are good that he would never be identified." She hesitated a moment, considering the possibilities. "If we hadn't stumbled on him, he would have died alone out there, and no one would have known his fate."

"At least we were able to report it," Terry said. "I'm sure they'll identify him sooner or later. Just the same, it was a gruesome sight, and I'm sorry that you had to see it."

"It certainly wasn't your fault. I'm just glad that we were able to help as much as we did."

"Well, we didn't find your turquoise."

"In light of everything that's happened, it doesn't seem so important. We can do it again some other time."

"I hope so," he said. "I'd hate to see you miss out on my expertise."

"Meaning that you'd like to show off for me, right?" she asked playfully.

"That could be." The line was momentarily silent.

"By the way," he continued, "I seem to recall that I missed your birthday a while back. I was wondering if I could take you to dinner to make up for it."

Allison restrained herself from accepting too quickly. Terry Braun was a man she felt she might like to get to know, but she had strong reservations about relationships. The phone was quiet in her ear.

"Well?" he said at last. "Are you still there?"

Allison chuckled. "I was just thinking about it."

"Thinking about it?"

"Well, you did miss my birthday, after all."

Terry laughed. "Don't forget, I'm paying."

"Where did you learn to sweet-talk a girl like that, Dr. Braun?" she teased.

He exhaled loudly with mock despair on the other end of the phone.

"I'd love to go," she said at last.

"Fine. How about tonight at the Crystal Palace? I'll pick you up at seven o'clock."

Allison's stomach lurched at the name. The Crystal Palace was one of the most elegant restaurants in the city. "Seven o'clock," she repeated.

"Great. I'll see you then."

Allison felt slightly conspicuous stepping from Terry's Jeep in the valet lot of the Crystal Palace. She didn't imagine that women generally arrived at the exclusive restaurant in four-wheel-drive vehicles.

She wore a sleek bustier dress of royal blue that accentuated her svelte figure. The fashionable basque waist accentuated her hips, and the deep color of the outfit was the perfect complement to her sapphire-blue eyes.

Terry wore an expensive-looking unconstructed blue sports jacket and a white cotton sports shirt, buttoned at the collar. His pants, too, were of white cotton, pleated, and cuffed. He radiated an air of fashionable modesty. He offered Allison his arm. "Shall we?" he asked.

"We shall," she replied, clasping his forearm.

They strolled the short distance to the front door and entered.

A distinguished-looking gentleman of middle age, dressed in a black tuxedo, approached them, and they were led to an intimate corner of the dimly lit restaurant.

Terry sat opposite Allison. A candle burning in the center of the small round table provided an air of romance to the occasion. Allison couldn't help but wonder about Terry's intentions. He seemed so rugged—not at all the type, she thought, to waste his time on the more subtle aspects of love.

Terry began to make small talk, commenting on the weather and the price of gasoline, but Allison only half listened. She eyed her surroundings as he spoke, taking in the elegance of the Crystal Palace. There was no doubt that Terry meant to impress her. And, she admitted, he was succeeding.

A waiter took their order for wine and appeared momentarily with two glasses and a bottle. He poured the wine expertly and placed the bottle in a gleaming silver bucket filled with small ice cubes.

Terry lifted his glass. "A toast," he said. "To a woman who doesn't lose her head under pressure."

Allison touched her glass to Terry's with a quiet chime and sipped at the wine. It was dry, and white, and not particularly tasty, she thought, which meant it was probably very expensive. She smiled over the rim of her glass. "That's good," she said.

Terry shook his head. "Seems a little bitter. You know, you're generally supposed to taste the wine before you buy it, but I wouldn't know if it tasted right or not."

"Really," Allison said, "it's fine."

"For all I know," Terry said, "it's *supposed* to taste like vinegar."

Allison set her glass on the table. "Am I to take it, then, that you're not delighted with the wine?"

"No, no, no, nothing like that." He glanced at the bottle, dripping with beads of moisture in the silver bucket. "At least I'll have something to pour on my salad."

"Well, I like it," Allison insisted.

"I guess that settles it, then."

Allison smiled at his wry humor. His lighthearted behavior seemed out of place in the classical ambience of the Crystal Palace. She found herself attracted to him.

Allison eyed her menu and was at once struck by the fact that no prices were listed. She knew that exclusive restaurants printed the prices only on menus distributed to those who were obviously paying for the meal.

The omission set Allison slightly on edge. She had never had much money as a child and had grown up respecting the value of a dollar. Even now, when by dint of her writing she was able to live comfortably, she still remembered the deprivations of her childhood and spent her money with care.

"Do you see anything that looks good?" Terry asked. His menu was cocked at an angle on the edge of the table. The prices, and they must have been exorbitant, didn't seem to concern him in the least.

Allison scanned the menu, carefully reading each listing and attempting to mentally calculate a list of prices. This was her first date with Terry, and she had no desire to order the most expensive dish on the menu.

Calves' feet and oysters. She shuddered at the thought and continued down the list. Veal chop with chanterelle mushrooms. That sounded interesting. Poached salmon with clam vinaigrette. Forget it, she thought. She had never been a fan of seafood, but buying it in the middle of the Arizona desert was utterly ridiculous. She continued reading the menu in silence.

At length Terry asked, "Have you decided?"

Allison smiled and folded her menu on the table. "I think so," she said. "The veal sounds good."

"All right." Terry nodded and glanced somewhere over her shoulder.

A waiter dressed in a tuxedo appeared immediately. "Are you ready to order?" he asked, his pen poised over an expensively bound pad.

Allison ordered the veal. The waiter wrote in his book with speedy efficiency. "And for you?" he asked Terry.

"That poached salmon in clam vinaigrette sounds good," he said.

"So it is, so it is," the waiter confirmed with a smile, penning the order in his pad.

Allison bit her lip to keep from smiling at the irony. The waiter finished writing up the order and left.

"I'm a real seafood nut," Terry said.

"Really?" Allison sipped her wine. "I've never really cared for it."

"I guess it comes from the time I lived up in Monterey. You know, Cannery Row and all."

"You lived in Monterey?" Allison asked with interest. She, too, had lived for a while near Monterey, in Salinas. But her memories of that time were unpleasant.

Terry seemed pleased at her interest and described how he had lived for a while selling souvenirs to tourists on Fisherman's Wharf. He hadn't made much money at it, but he had managed to survive, for what he described as the best summer of his life, on the profits his little booth had netted.

The conversation drifted on. Allison found Terry to be well read and was surprised to learn that he shared her affection for Steinbeck and Hemingway.

The conversation was lively and entertaining and continued after their food had arrived. She told him about her aspirations as a teenager to become a world-class ballerina, and he seemed genuinely interested when she described the arduous training required for the ballet.

Terry talked at length about Allison's writing. Though she maintained an even composure while talking about her work, she was secretly thrilled that he was interested in her career.

"As a matter of fact," she said, attempting to sound

offhand, "I'm trying to write a novel these days." In fact, he was the only one to whom she had confessed this.

"Is that right?" he asked, leaning forward. "Sounds like a serious undertaking. What is it going to be about?"

Immediately she regretted mentioning the book. For all the hours she had spent at her computer, she had a painfully small stack of pages completed. She wasn't even sure that a plot was developing. Finishing the work at this point seemed an impossible task.

She laughed self-deprecatingly at his question. "To tell you the truth," she answered, "I don't know. So far it's just a small pile of paper."

Terry smiled. "Think I could read it?"

"You'll have to wait until it's finished. Just like everyone else."

"Even if I know the author?" He glanced at the bottle of wine, resting untouched in the silver bucket. The ice had begun to melt, and the tiny beads of moisture on the bottle's neck had evaporated. "We haven't even touched the wine," he said, pulling the bottle free and tilting it over Allison's glass. "Would you care for some more?" he asked, already pouring.

"That's fine." Allison remembered the bitter taste and attempted to wave the bottle off gracefully. "I really don't want any more."

"Go ahead. It's all yours."

"Thanks, but I think I've had enough."

"You've only had one glass," Terry countered as he finished pouring.

"That's right."

"And that's enough?"

Allison shrugged.

"But I thought you said you liked it."

Allison smiled. "I lied."

They laughed out loud.

Chapter Three

*T*he long-distance connection buzzed, popped, and echoed. Allison strained to hear through the interference as the sheriff's deputy in Kingman reported what had been learned about the old man.

His name, she discovered, had been Esteban Montoya, and he had journeyed north to the desert outside Kingman from his home in Nogales, Mexico.

She glanced absently at her clock as a strong burst of static cut through the line. Eleven-fifteen. ". . . had apparently been wandering around in the desert for several days," the deputy was saying.

"Do you have any leads on a possible murderer?" Allison asked.

"Excuse me?" The deputy's voice sounded as though he were talking through a narrow pipe.

Allison repeated her question slowly, in a loud tone of voice.

"A murderer," the deputy repeated, as though he were trying to recall what she was talking about. "Oh, that." Something that may have been laughter echoed over the wire. "The only murderer out in that desert was the sun," he said.

"Then you don't think Mr. Montoya was intentionally killed?"

"How's that?"

Allison took a deep breath and repeated her question.

"Like we told you when you made the report. . . ." Another burst of static cut the line. ". . . delirious from the sun and heat. They say just about anything."

Allison was certain that she had missed no vital information during the static burst and so did not ask the officer to repeat his response. The heat and delirium were responsible for the man's ramblings. Yet he had been insistent that Allison contact his wife, and she had given him her word that she would do so.

"Did you locate his wife?" Allison asked. "He wanted me to relay a message to her."

"His wife—yeah, just a minute." The line was dead, except for some electronic clicks and pops as the deputy searched for the address. "Here it is," he said, returning to the phone. "Rosa Montoya. Age, sixty-seven." He read her address to Allison.

Allison penciled the information into a pad she kept handy beside her phone, thanked the officer, and hung up.

She fell back into her sofa and examined the words she had just written. *Rosa Montoya.* She tried to imagine how the woman might look, what type of home she kept, how many children she had. She stared at the name on the paper but could derive no answers to her questions. She wondered how long Esteban and Rosa had been married; then she remembered Esteban's

dying request. *"Tell Rosa I love her."* She knew what had to be done.

She set the notepad on the end table beside the phone, crossed to her converted office, and rummaged in her desk for her address book. She flipped through the pages and searched the B's.

Strange, she thought, that she should have to look for Terry Braun's number. She ran her finger over the page, across the names of several people with whom she had once had business dealings but who would probably never remember her now. There—Terry Braun, PhD, geology professor, Arizona State University. She read the number, which rang his office at the university. The memory of her dinner with him returned momentarily. Someday, she thought, she might want to get his home number.

She smiled as she recalled the previous evening. The conversation had been light and fun. Exactly what she had needed after the ordeal in the desert. Terry was funny and kind. And, she recalled significantly, he had asked her if she was involved with anyone. She had hedged the question.

She dialed Terry's number. He had appeared to be interested in getting to know her on closer terms, but she was wary of his advances. She had her own reasons to distrust men. She rubbed the thought from her mind as his phone began to ring.

"Dr. Braun," he answered. He sounded authoritative yet friendly. Allison couldn't help but smile.

She told him about the phone call she had placed to the sheriff's office in Kingman and what she had learned about the old man.

"That was fast," Terry said when she had finished. "I guess that gold cap really did come in handy."

"I was wondering," Allison began. She paused for a moment. "I gave Esteban my word that I would see his wife and—"

"You want to visit her in Nogales?"

"I really think I should."

"Maybe you're right," Terry said. "It might be awkward, though. What will you say?"

"I'm not sure. I really hadn't thought about it. I'll just tell her that her husband was thinking about her. That he loved her." Again she was moved by the realization that the dying man's final thoughts had concerned his love for his wife. She wondered whether her father had ever thought about her mother.

"A visit would be a nice gesture," Terry was saying.

"I was wondering if you would like to come along. I would feel awkward simply showing up on Rosa Montoya's doorstep alone."

"For moral support?" Terry asked.

"That's right." But deep down Allison knew that her answer wasn't completely accurate. True, Terry would be able to lend some moral support, but she had weathered more uncomfortable encounters in her career as a writer. She realized that she wanted him to go with her simply for the sake of company.

"I'm a little busy today," Terry said. "Would tomorrow be all right?"

"Fine."

"I'll swing around to pick you up in the morning then—say, ten o'clock?"

"I'll be ready," Allison promised.

*   *   *

The drive to Nogales took almost six hours. Allison and Terry stopped along the way in Tucson for lunch before completing their journey across the border.

Terry navigated his Jeep slowly through the crowded streets of the Mexican city. Traffic snaked crazily through the narrow lanes, oblivious to any order. On street corners, taco vendors and trinket dealers haggled over the price of their wares with tourists crossing the border from Arizona.

A horn honked angrily, and Terry slammed his brakes. The Jeep lurched to a halt only inches from a blue compact that was swerving madly through the midafternoon traffic, scarcely slowing for other vehicles or pedestrians.

"Crazy place," Terry commented, easing forward slowly from the near collision.

"You almost need eyes in the back of your head," Allison agreed.

The Jeep crawled along the jammed street. Terry surveyed the congested roadway and scouted street signs. He nodded at one marking an intersection. "Can you make that out?" he asked.

Allison squinted her eyes against the glare of sun reflecting off the silver sign and read the name of the street, spelled in black letters. "It means Center Street," she said.

"What's the address we're hunting for?" he asked, coasting to a stop to allow a vendor pushing a two-wheeled cart laden with leather belts to struggle slowly across the street.

Allison's eyes drifted to the paper in her lap, though

she had memorized the address long ago. "It's on a street called El Parque."

Terry touched the accelerator lightly, and the Jeep inched forward. "Something tells me that we're not going to just accidentally run into Rosa Montoya's house."

Allison surveyed the apparent mass confusion on the street. A battered pickup truck laden with rubber tires was stalled crossways in the road. Clouds of steam issued from under the hood. The driver stood on the road, watching his truck overheat and scratching his head. Traffic was at a snarled standstill; while irate drivers honked their horns, pedestrians took advantage of the lull in traffic to cross the street.

"I don't feel like getting stuck in that," Terry said, indicating the knot of traffic growing around the stalled pickup. He cut the wheel and turned the Jeep up a narrow alley that ran between two rows of red-brick buildings.

Pedestrians opened a pathway for the Jeep as Terry guided the vehicle over a curb and into the alley. "Hope we fit," he said, hunching forward over the wheel and gauging the width of the alley.

He inched the Jeep into the opening with a sigh of relief.

"Just about one inch to spare," Allison noted as the Jeep moved up the alley.

Terry maintained a watchful eye on the red-brick walls until the Jeep emerged from the alley onto a street that was nearly as congested as the one they had just left.

"There," Allison said, pointing at a white, modern-looking structure. The Mexican flag flew lazily atop a flagpole before the building. "A police station. They should be able to guide us to El Parque."

Terry guided the Jeep to a stop in front of the police station, and they entered the building.

They were greeted by a slim officer seated at a desk in the lobby. *"Buenos días,"* he said, his tone and manner bespeaking his official position.

Allison answered him in Spanish and asked for directions to Rosa Montoya's home.

The officer's official demeanor lightened somewhat as Allison spoke. It was evident that he appreciated her use of his native language. He brought a map from one of his desk drawers, flattened it atop the desk, and pointed out the route to El Parque.

Allison wrote the instructions carefully in a small spiral notebook and thanked the officer.

He smiled brightly and offered his hand in turn to her and Terry. "Have an enjoyable stay in our city," he said, speaking in accented English.

Rosa Montoya lived in a small home of rough planking on the southern edge of the city. Her house was bordered on either side by vacant lots, but a large, red-brick apartment building occupied nearly the entire length of the opposite side of the street.

Allison and Terry knocked on the front door and waited.

A faint rustling inside the house met their ears; then the sound of footsteps grew clear. The door opened, and Rosa Montoya faced her two visitors.

She appeared to be momentarily puzzled by the appearance of the two Americans on her front doorstep; then realization slowly edged into her features.

Allison smiled and introduced herself and Terry. Rosa Montoya appeared much older than she had expected. Allison immediately wondered about the wisdom of appearing unannounced so shortly after Mr. Montoya's death.

"Please," Rosa Montoya said in Spanish, standing aside. "Come in."

Allison and Terry entered the small home. The floors were wooden and gleamed brightly from years of use. A large fan oscillated back and forth atop a bookcase lined with encyclopedias. The furniture was old but in good repair. A large picture window looked out onto the street. Family photographs stared into the room from the walls. A black-and-white television flickered from a corner of the living room. Rosa switched it off and settled into a wooden rocking chair. "Please, sit," she offered, indicating a sofa in the center of the room.

Allison settled into the sofa, and Terry sat beside her. Allison smiled kindly at the old woman. "Señora Montoya," she said, "I regret the sad circumstances that have brought us together."

Mrs. Montoya attempted a smile and nodded. "I know the reason for your visit. The police gave me the names of the two Americans who found my Esteban in the desert."

Allison hesitated. The speech she had been planning on the trip down somehow didn't fit the situation. Her hours of mental rehearsal had transformed her true emotions into a packaged speech. She decided to discard her preplanned words and searched for something to say. "I'm so sorry," she said. "I know that it is impossible for words alone to soothe your heartache at a time like this."

"It is a difficult period for me," Rosa Montoya allowed. She glanced at Terry, who sat stiffly beside Allison. "Does your friend speak Spanish?" she asked. She laughed quietly when Terry didn't respond to her question, and before Allison could answer said, in English, "I lived in El Paso for several years when I was a young lady. I think it will be more comfortable for all if we speak in English."

Allison was impressed by the older woman's composure. She repeated her condolences and relayed Esteban Montoya's dying message to his wife. "He wanted me to tell you that he loved you," she said softly, her voice filled with comfort.

Rosa Montoya's eyes filled with tears. She sniffed quietly, and Terry was immediately on his feet, offering her a handkerchief. She dabbed at her eyes but continued to cry softly. Terry placed a hand on her shoulder. From outside, the happy sounds of children playing in the street could be heard.

"I'm sorry," he said. His eyes held a deep sincerity.

"There is nothing anyone could have done." Rosa's voice was a bare whisper.

"We tried," Allison assured her.

"He insisted on going," Mrs. Montoya said. "Insisted. Even after our son. . . ." Her voice trailed away. To Allison, the ensuing silence bespoke a grief too deep for tears.

Terry patted her shoulder.

"I knew that he would not return," she said at last.

"His death comes as no surprise. I only wish. . . ." She again lapsed into silence.

The room was heavy with the silence of the widow's grieving. Terry and Allison waited sympathetically.

Mrs. Montoya seemed to be wrestling with herself. She glanced at Allison and seemed about to speak before suddenly averting her face and staring into her lap.

She sat that way, in silence, for several seconds, wringing the handkerchief through her fingers. Finally, in a voice that was almost inaudible, she said, "It was the same way for my son." She drew her attention from her lap and gazed for a long moment at Allison. "He, too, was killed in the desert. Six months ago."

Killed. Allison was stunned. She noticed the surprised look on Terry's face.

Mrs. Montoya's face reflected an infinite sadness but a firmness of belief. "You think I am crazy?" she asked. "Like all the others. They say I am crazy too. Just a crazy old woman. *Loco.*"

"No," Allison said quickly. "I don't think you're crazy."

"What do you mean, killed?" Terry asked.

Mrs. Montoya nodded in his direction. "Maybe it is *you* who will say that I am *loco.*"

"No," Terry insisted. "No. I don't think you're crazy."

"Your husband tried to mention someone," Allison interrupted.

Mrs. Montoya's eyes widened with interest. "A name?" she asked.

"I didn't think it was important," Allison said.

"Whose name?" Mrs. Montoya asked, her voice growing stronger.

"We thought it was because of . . . we thought he was. . . ." Allison searched for words. "We thought he was delirious . . . because of his condition."

"What name?" Mrs. Montoya insisted.

"He didn't mention a name, really."

"What did he say?"

Allison hesitated. "Only a letter," she said at last. "P."

Mrs. Montoya's face collapsed in grief, and she buried her face in the handkerchief. "The Evil One," she said, sobbing.

Chapter Four

*T*erry glanced at Allison. His expression showed a mixture of surprise and interest. He waited for several seconds until the grieving woman had regained her composure, then asked, "Do you know the name your husband was trying to say?"

Mrs. Montoya spoke so quietly that Allison was forced to lean forward in her seat to make out the words.

"Pablo Ramirez," she said. "He and his brother own the land on which our house stands."

"If you suspect him of murder, you must inform the police," Allison urged.

Mrs. Montoya laughed grimly. "You do not know Nogales. I would invite trouble simply by accusing the Ramirez brothers. They are close friends with the police. In any event, the killer is clever. He has arranged for his work to appear as accidents. There is no evidence of murder."

She cried softly as she spoke. "Six months ago my son vanished. Of course, we suspected foul play. It was too much of a coincidence for him to disappear while

36

searching for the treasure." Her breath trembled. "He was to be married soon," she said, biting at her bottom lip. Her face quivered with sorrow.

"Then, when my Esteban decided to conduct the search himself, he told me that he felt he was being constantly followed. He told me that his search for the treasure could mean great danger. He did not know who was following him. But things happened, strange things. Our dog was poisoned. Our windows broken. 'Beware,' he warned me. 'Beware the Evil One.' "

"The Evil One?" Allison asked.

Mrs. Montoya nodded. "It is what he called the stranger who followed him. The Evil One." A forlorn expression crossed her face, and she dabbed at her eyes with the handkerchief. She glanced up at Terry. "It is because of the gold," she told him. "Come, sit beside your friend. I will tell you about it if you wish to hear."

Terry settled into the sofa next to Allison. He gripped his hands to his knees and studied Mrs. Montoya intently. "Your husband did mention gold," he said. "But the area where he was found no longer holds any."

Mrs. Montoya nodded. "There is gold. My husband believed so, and my son." She bit her lip. "Francisco." She indicated a photo on the wall. "We called him Pancho."

Allison listened quietly as she spoke. Now Mrs. Montoya's eyes took on a faraway look as she silently recalled people and places from her past.

At last she spoke. "It is dangerous," she said, "what I am about to tell you. I do not know what the price has been in lost lives, but I know the suffering this information has caused for me." She stared at Allison. "Do you wish to accept the risk?"

The question seemed to relay both a threat and a warning, and it slightly unnerved Allison. She had encountered risky business in her years as a reporter but never anything as blatantly dangerous as outright murder. She hesitated before answering.

Suddenly she realized that she had no choice. If a murderer really was on the prowl and if he had taken the lives of Esteban Montoya and his son, then he needed to be captured. The police were doing nothing. Indeed, they did not even believe that any crimes had been committed.

Allison faced Mrs. Montoya. "I want to hear your story," she said, reaching into her purse and withdrawing the small, spiral-bound notebook in which she had written the directions to the Montoya home.

"You are young and beautiful and have much to look forward to in your life," Mrs. Montoya intoned. "Are you certain?"

Allison flipped to a blank page. "I'm certain."

"And you?" Mrs. Montoya asked, turning her attention to Terry. "Do you dare risk your life, simply to hear a tale that may be no more than myth?"

Terry smiled, as if to shrug off the element of danger. "I don't think that simply listening could cause any harm."

Mrs. Montoya's face grew stern. "Do not make light of this," she warned. "The Evil One knows. He watches and he hears. Do you risk knowing the information that has caused so much sadness?"

Terry assumed a serious pose. "I want to hear your story."

"Even now," Mrs. Montoya cautioned, "the Evil One may be watching."

The thought made Allison slightly uneasy. "Then he knows where you live?" she asked.

"I cannot say for certain, for I do not know where he gets his information. I can say only this. The man is a phantom. He hides in the shadows and watches and waits. If he is watching my house at this moment, then he has seen you enter, and he will wonder about the nature of your visit."

"But you haven't told us anything yet," Allison said. Mrs. Montoya's words were making her anxious.

"How will he be sure?" Mrs. Montoya asked rhetorically. "He will learn that you have been here. Even by arriving at my front door you have placed yourself in jeopardy. It is a rare thing for Yankees to appear in this neighborhood."

"You have done a fine job of warning us," Terry interrupted, sounding slightly irritated. "But if, as you say, we have placed ourselves in danger by visiting you, then perhaps you could tell us why such a danger exists, so we would at least know what we were up against."

Mrs. Montoya smiled wryly. "You are impatient. It is the disease of youth. I was young once myself, and I know." The faraway look returned to her eyes as she lapsed into a period of silent reminiscence.

Suddenly her face hardened, and a stern expression crossed her features. "But there is no need for this old woman to waste any more of your time. I will tell you the story of the Confederate gold. It may be truth, it may be fiction. I do not know. It may bring you great wealth and joy, or it may bring you. . . ." She gestured to the photos on the wall. Pancho had been a handsome young man with black, shoulder-length hair and dark, penetrating eyes. Esteban Montoya smiled proudly. "Or it may bring you heartache and despair."

Allison interrupted. "We may be able to locate the Evil One and put him in prison."

Mrs. Montoya nodded. "That is good. But nothing can ever make up for the sadness this tale has visited upon my family." A long period of silence followed; then she concluded, "I am the only one now."

The fan atop the bookshelf swung slowly across the room, washing Allison with a momentary breath of cool air. Through the front window children could be seen playing in the street.

"You know about the Battle at Picacho Peak?" Mrs. Montoya asked suddenly.

The question took Allison by surprise, and she was forced to hesitate a moment as she tried to place what Mrs. Montoya was talking about.

"The Civil War battle," Mrs. Montoya reminded them, reading the confusion on their faces.

"Oh, that's right," Allison suddenly said. Mention of the Civil War had jogged her memory. The Battle of Picacho Peak had been fought at a mountain slightly north of Tucson. The skirmish had taken no lives and counted as the only battle of the Civil War to have been fought on Arizona soil.

Terry nodded. "I've read about it."

Mrs. Montoya continued. "Then you know that the southern half of Arizona claimed loyalty to the Confed-

eracy during the Civil War and that the northern half
was aligned with the North?"

"Yes." Allison nodded. "But I believe Arizona was
only a territory at the time, not a state."

"You are right," Mrs. Montoya said. "It was not a
state. And, also, it was far removed from the intense
fighting. These two factors led some in the Confederacy
to believe that the Arizona Territory would be the perfect location to continue their struggle for indepen-
dence."

"To continue their struggle?" Terry asked. "What do
you mean?"

"The period I speak of occurred near the end of your
Civil War, when all but the most fanatical in the Confederacy had sacrificed any hope of victory. These rebels saw the Arizona Territory as the new frontier for
their struggle. Since Arizona was not a state, they
thought that the Union would not hold a tight claim
on the land. And since the territory was located in the
vast deserts to the west, defending the area would have
been difficult, indeed."

Allison listened intently. "So these renegades in the
Confederate Army considered abandoning the struggle
in the Deep South, and moving it into Arizona."

"*Sí,*" Mrs. Montoya said. "The location of the territory met their needs. But there was still one more fac-
tor, a very important one, that was taken into consider-
ation before final preparations were made." She
hesitated and eyed her two listeners.

"What was that?" Terry asked.

"You are familiar with the fact that England supplied
the Confederacy during the Civil War?" she asked.

"But the Union blockaded the Southern ports," Terry answered, "and was able to strangle the South."

"That is correct," Mrs. Montoya said. "And now you will understand why it is important to remember that Arizona borders on Mexico." She paused. "The Confederate extremists realized that they would be able to funnel supplies across the border without any fear of interruption."

Allison was puzzled. "I'm afraid I don't understand."

"In order to prevent the supplies from reaching Confederates in Arizona," Mrs. Montoya said, "the Union would have had to blockade Mexico."

"And," Terry said, sounding almost triumphant, "blockading Mexico would have been an act of war."

Mrs. Montoya nodded. "The Union could not risk another war. They were just concluding the bloodiest in their history."

"So these Confederate radicals felt that, having lost in the East and the South, they would be able to win the war in the West," Allison stated.

"It sounds that way," Terry assented. "But it's obvious that nothing ever happened with their plans." He glanced at Mrs. Montoya, sitting quietly in her rocking chair. "Why?" he asked. "What happened?"

"That is where the story of the Confederate gold begins."

Terry and Allison leaned forward with expectation. But Mrs. Montoya had her own way of relating things.

"It is strange, is it not, that those things which once caused a family shame and embarrassment should later be cause for pride?" she asked.

"In what way?" Allison asked politely.

"I have recently read about a man who claims to be a descendant of John Wilkes Booth, the man who assassinated your President Lincoln. One hundred years ago this man would have been disgraced by the actions of his relative. He would have gone to great lengths to hide his relationship with the assassin."

Allison smiled and nodded. "Time passes and things change. A claim to notoriety is distinguishing. Not many people are able to claim either greatness or evil in their family tree."

Mrs. Montoya closed her eyes, a smile on her face. "It is curious, no?" She opened her eyes and leaned forward, looking at Allison. "My husband's family was what you might call distinguished," she said with a wry smile.

"In what way?" Terry asked.

"Pedro Montoya, my husband's grandfather, was a *bandido.*"

"An outlaw?" Terry asked.

"A very good outlaw," Mrs. Montoya corrected. "He and his gang raided along the border with Arizona, robbing banks, stealing horses, and holding up any who strayed into their territory."

Allison said, "Your family has the distinction of claiming a *bandido* in its past."

Mrs. Montoya laughed a short laugh. "That is right. These things have happened long ago, so I may tell of it now with pride."

Terry and Allison smiled with her.

She laced her fingers together and dropped her hands into her lap. "Pedro Montoya and his gang robbed a shipment of gold destined for the Confederate rebels in Arizona," she said. "The shipment had arrived from England at the port city of Tampico, on the Gulf of Mexico. It was a huge shipment and was to be used by the Confederate renegades to purchase arms and to bribe the Indians in the Arizona Territory to fight on the side of the Confederacy.

"The gold was hauled by mule train overland to Nogales, here, in Mexico, under guard of the Mexican Army, and was deposited in a bank vault until the Confederate agents in Arizona could provide transportation for the treasure across the border.

"Finally a small company of Confederate loyalists arrived in Nogales. The Governor General refused to turn the treasure over to the rebels, claiming that they did not possess the manpower to protect the shipment. The Confederates demanded the gold and threatened to notify England if the money was not turned over to them.

"The Governor General did not wish to excite an altercation between the Governments of Mexico and England, but he knew that he was responsible for the safety of the gold until it crossed the border into the Arizona Territory. At last he agreed to turn the treasure over to the rebels, but only on the condition that they accept a contingent of Mexican Army guards to escort them the few remaining miles to the Arizona border, a condition to which the rebels immediately agreed."

Allison and Terry sat spellbound by the tale. Neither spoke as Mrs. Montoya continued.

"The mule train left Nogales in the early morning of October 12, 1864. The movement of the gold had been top secret, and there is no doubt that the secrecy had been enforced. It was purely coincidence that the company of Mexican soldiers and Confederate rebels should have crossed paths with Pedro Montoya's gang less than one mile from the Arizona border.

"Montoya's men realized that the highly guarded mule train probably contained a great treasure. They were fearless men, toughened by years of life in the cruel desert. Most of them had a price on their head. They felt that they had nothing to lose. And, of course, they were thieves, so they attacked the convoy."

Mrs. Montoya took a deep breath and eyed her listeners. "There were many killed," she said. "On both sides. But in the end Pedro Montoya's gang escaped with the treasure."

Allison glanced at Terry, who was leaning forward in his seat, mesmerized by the tale.

Mrs. Montoya continued. "Because he had murdered Mexican officers and because he had stolen hundreds of thousands of dollars' worth of gold that had been entrusted to the care of the Mexican government, the Mexican Army was called into the search. Mexico was a very unsafe place for Pedro Montoya, and he knew it, so he left his wife and son and headed north.

"But he was hunted in southern Arizona by the Confederate renegades, whose gold he had plundered. He had no illusions about his fate should he fall into their hands, so he continued ever farther north, to the very border of the Arizona Territory, near the mining town of Kingman.

"Along the way, many of his gang mutinied, and much of the treasure was taken by deserters who stole before they fled into the desert. Still more gold was divided up among the loyal members of the gang, who finally disbanded in Kingman.

"Whatever became of all the treasure, I cannot say, but Pedro Montoya, as leader of the gang, reserved, by his estimation, tens of thousands of dollars' worth of gold."

Terry leaped from his seat and paced the floor in front of the sofa. He glanced at Allison, then at Mrs. Montoya, then back to Allison. "Tens of thousands of dollars," he said. Then he repeated it. "Tens of thousands of dollars." He stopped shortly and fixed Allison with his gaze. His eyes shone with excitement. "Don't you see?" he asked, forcing himself to contain his energy. "That was tens of thousands of dollars' worth of gold in 1864. The price has skyrocketed since then. We could be talking about hundreds of thousands of dollars, maybe even millions."

Allison listened with quiet skepticism.

"That is correct, Señor Braun," Mrs. Montoya said.

Allison interrupted. "If the gold exists, why didn't Pedro Montoya simply retrieve it?"

Mrs. Montoya nodded. "The story seems hard to believe, does it not? Yet my husband believed, and his father before him." She lapsed into a short silence.

"The Confederate rebels lost the support of England when the gold was stolen. Maybe the English believed that the Arizona Territory was too hostile to be able to ensure that their supplies would be delivered. Maybe they never believed that the gold was stolen in the first place. No matter their reasons, the English ceased support for the rebels in Arizona.

"So, you see, Pedro Montoya was a man without a country. The Mexican officials wanted him dead, as did the Confederate rebels in southern Arizona. His previous criminal record haunted him as well, for he had committed many crimes in Arizona. He no longer had the security of his gang, and though he had much gold, its very weight slowed him down. He required several mules to transport it. He was forced to hide most of it somewhere in northern Arizona, near Kingman. In a cave. He lived the remainder of his life on the run."

"But surely," Allison said, "others learned of the location of the gold."

"Why should they?" Mrs. Montoya asked almost incredulously. "Pedro Montoya was a *bandido*. He protected his treasure."

"Then how do you know it exists?" Allison asked, hoping that the question didn't sound as rude as it seemed, but wanting to get at the truth of the matter.

Terry had stopped his pacing and was standing beside the window at the front of the room. The children had vanished from the street outside.

"One year after the robbery," Mrs. Montoya explained, "Pedro Montoya returned to his family in the town of Magdalena. He carried with him a crude map he had drawn, showing the location of the treasure north of Kingman. He entrusted the map to his wife, for he was heading for safety in New Mexico, and was certain that he would see neither his family nor the treasure again.

"He was wounded in a shootout in Agua Prieta as he made his way toward New Mexico and for some reason changed his plans. He was last seen in Kingman, very weak from his injury, several days later. The gold has never been recovered."

Allison sat silently, digesting what she had just heard. The story made sense. It was possible that a top-secret shipment of gold could have been intercepted by a gang of bandits and that a portion of that gold could have been secreted near Kingman. The story was neat and tidy. But suspicion lingered. Seldom in her career as a free-lance writer had she encountered stories that were so easily wrapped up.

"Do you have the map?" she asked.

Mrs. Montoya hesitated. "I do not have it," she said, "but I have seen it. For many years we kept it here, in the house, but it is gone now." Apparently noticing the look of skepticism on Allison's face, she quickly added, "Just before he was killed, my husband hid the map in a place only he would know. With the Evil One on his trail, he thought I would be safer if I knew nothing of its location."

"Then you have no proof of the map's existence," Allison stated, feeling as though the entire story she had just heard was a hoax.

Mrs. Montoya picked up on Allison's incredulity. "My son, Pancho, saw the map as well. He used it in his search, before he was. . . ."

Allison was immediately sorry for having doubted her word.

"After Pancho was murdered, my husband moved the map from the house and hid it." Mrs. Montoya crossed to the bookshelf. She ran her fingernail under the edge of the topmost shelf and pulled a thin strip of wood. A small, hollowed-out space appeared. "The map had been hidden here until then," she said.

Allison and Terry eyed the tiny vault.

"If the map was in your husband's family for so many years," Terry asked, "why is it that no one began searching for the gold until now?"

"You must believe the danger," Mrs. Montoya intoned. "My husband's father lived at a time when many members of the original gang still roamed the desert. They knew of Pedro Montoya's gold, and they watched his family, ready to attack like mad dogs if any of the money should ever appear.

"My husband was not an educated man, but he was very wise. He knew the heartache the treasure had created and the many deaths it had caused. He kept the map a secret from his own son until a few months ago. He understood well the passions in a young man's heart. And he understood Pancho's fierce pride." She paused for a moment of silent reminiscence and smiled to herself. "He would brag about everything."

She again fixed her attention on her audience. "Knowledge of gold treasure would have been a difficult secret for him to keep. I am certain that Esteban would have delayed telling him of it had not the Ramirez brothers, who own the land upon which our home is built, threatened to take our land from us.

"You see, we own our home but must lease our land from the Ramirez brothers. It has always been so. The Ramirez family owns this land. Our lease expires in two months, and the Ramirez brothers will not allow us to renew it. They own the apartments across the street, and they want this land to build more."

"By law, they must offer us the option to buy the land when the lease expires, but we do not have any money. We cannot move our house. . . ." She bit her bottom lip and tried to blink back tears. "We will lose everything if we do not buy." She wiped her eyes. "They demanded a huge sum. I am an old woman, no? And Esteban an old man. We could not stand to move from the only home in which we had ever lived.

"Esteban told Pancho of the treasure and had him memorize the map. He hoped our son would be able to locate it. Somehow the Evil One—perhaps a descendant of one of the gang members, like my son himself, or perhaps Pablo Ramirez—learned of the gold. Pancho left to search for the treasure six months ago and was never seen again. It is not difficult to imagine that the Evil One discovered his trail and—" She bit her knuckle, and a tear edged over her cheek.

She stopped speaking for a moment, and the room was cloaked in silence.

"When Pancho was killed, Esteban said he no longer had use for the map. He had memorized it years earlier and had kept it in the house only so his son might learn of the legend."

"What did he do with the map?" Terry asked, running his finger along the bookshelf.

Mrs. Montoya smiled faintly. "He said he wanted to hide it where anyone might be able to find it."

"Where *anyone* could find it? But why?" Allison asked.

"Esteban said that the Evil One had gone to great lengths to get the map. He thought it would be justice to place the map in such a location that whoever might find it would be able to easily locate the treasure."

"Where did he hide it?" Allison asked.

Mrs. Montoya studied Allison with a severe expression. "Do you intend to hunt for the lost gold?"

"I intend to get to the bottom of the mystery," she said. "To learn the truth behind the deaths of your son and husband."

"I am afraid that you will not like my husband's choice of hiding places."

"Where is it?" Allison asked.

When Mrs. Montoya answered, Allison's jaw dropped in disbelief. She glanced at Terry, whose face mirrored her own surprise.

Chapter Five

*T*erry squatted beside his Jeep and surveyed the flat tire. "The valve stem's been cut," he said, standing up and wiping his hands clean on the thighs of his pants.

"Why would anyone do that?" Allison asked, tilting her head slightly to see past Terry and examine the tire lying folded under the chrome rim.

He walked past her and began loosening the spare tire from the rack on the rear hatch. "How would I know?" His voice held a testy edge. "We're going to have to get it fixed before we go anywhere."

The Jeep was still parked in front of Mrs. Montoya's home. They had discovered that the front driver's-side tire had been flattened while they had been inside speaking with Mrs. Montoya.

A group of children suddenly appeared at the end of the street. Terry tugged the spare free of the rack and let it bounce to the ground. "Probably those kids," he said, rolling the tire forward.

"How can you say that?" Allison asked, slightly irritated by his accusatory tone.

"Who else could it have been?"

Allison shrugged and tried to sound offhand, but the conversation inside Mrs. Montoya's home and her warnings concerning the Evil One played on her thoughts. "Maybe someone was watching us."

"Oh, come on. You don't really buy all that hokum, do you?"

"Why shouldn't I?" she asked indignantly. "The story made perfect sense, and someone or something *did* kill Mr. Montoya and his son."

Terry turned to the Jeep's cargo area and fished through a collection of antifreeze containers and oil cans before emerging with a jack and a lug wrench. "The only people responsible for Esteban's and Pancho's deaths are Esteban and Pancho. The desert is no place to embark on wild-goose chases for mythical gold."

The sound of children's voices grew louder as the tight knot of kids grew closer.

"So you think everything we just heard is nonsense?" Allison asked, following Terry to the deflated front tire.

He hunched over and placed the jack under the Jeep. "Nonsense isn't quite the word I would use," he said, twisting the jack handle. "Malarkey is much better." The Jeep raised slightly as the jack made contact with the chassis.

Terry used the lug wrench to loosen the lug nuts. "What about that crazy map story?" he asked, turning slightly to face Allison over his shoulder. "Hiding a priceless map, a map containing a key to a fortune in gold, hiding that map in a book in the Phoenix City Library. What kind of bunk is that? And why is it that she doesn't even know the title of the book in which it's hidden?"

Allison was about to answer when the children who had been walking down the street swarmed around the disabled Jeep. She estimated that there were more than twelve children in all, ranging in age from about five to fourteen.

One especially pretty girl, dressed in a pink dress and white shoes, approached Allison and smiled brightly. A tiny gap showed where she had lost one of her teeth. "Hello," she said in highly accented English and giggled.

Terry had loosened all the lug nuts and was removing them with his fingers. "Watch them," he warned quietly.

"Oh, you," Allison answered. "Get back to fixing the tire."

The children milled about the Jeep noisily, chattering among themselves and laughing and giggling. Allison assumed that they were interested in the Jeep and allowed them to open the doors and peer inside.

"*¿Qué tal?*" she asked one boy. "How are you?"

The boy averted his gaze and stared self-consciously at his sneakers. Allison mussed his hair gently and watched an older boy on the other side of the Jeep examining the interior through the open passenger door.

Suddenly two girls ran up on either side of Allison, grabbed her wrists, and started jabbering in Spanish. "Look out for your watch," Terry said, standing from the fender and eyeing the fray closely.

"You don't trust anyone, do you?" Allison asked

pointedly, glancing down at the smiling faces of the little girls.

"And that's why," Terry shouted, pointing at the youth who had been peering through the passenger door. He had snagged Allison's notebook from the seat and was running away with it down the street. "Get back here," Terry shouted. He tried to chase the boy, but to no avail. The remaining children swarmed around him, making it impossible for him to break free without the possibility of causing an injury.

Allison wriggled free from the girls and watched the boy disappear through the space between two wings of the apartment building across the street.

"He's got your notebook," Terry said as he vanished.

Allison shrugged. "It's empty. I didn't take any notes in the house."

As quickly as they had appeared, the children regrouped and ran down the street.

Terry squatted down at the fender and completed jacking up the Jeep. "They could have taken your watch," he said.

Allison looked inside the Jeep. "Or my purse," she commented, noting that her purse lay where she had placed it on the floorboards.

Terry grunted as he yanked the useless tire free.

"Don't you think it's strange," Allison asked, "that those kids suddenly appeared like that?"

"They were working a rip-off," Terry said.

"I was able to figure that much out myself," she replied and, eyeing the poverty in the neighborhood, she could understand the motivation. "But they didn't steal my purse. They only went for the notebook."

Terry lifted the spare onto the axle and started to finger-tighten the lug nuts. "Maybe it was the first thing the kid saw."

"No," Allison said, considering the situation. "My purse was in plain view. He knew what he wanted, and he wanted the notebook."

Terry didn't speak as he lowered the front end of the car.

"I was carrying the notebook when we left the house," Allison reminded him. "Anyone watching us would surely have seen it."

"And who would have been watching us?" he asked, turning the wrench on the lug nuts.

She hesitated. She felt silly saying it, but finally she said, "The Evil One."

"Huh." Terry leaned into the last of the lug nuts and retrieved the jack from under the car. "You think this evil guy staked us out and hired those kids to steal your notebook, just in case you'd filled it with any good information?" He returned to the cargo bay of the Jeep and replaced the tools.

"Well, it makes sense," Allison argued.

"So does circumstance." He hefted the useless tire off the roadway and tossed it into the cargo bay. "Those kids just happened to come by when we were fixing the tire." His face suddenly lit up. "That's it," he said more to himself than to Allison. He faced her. "They cut the valve stem on the tire because they knew we would have to fix it before we could leave. Then they staked out the Jeep until we returned, and when we did, they made off with the first thing they could find." He slammed the cargo door shut to emphasize his statement.

"It's possible," Allison conceded. Perhaps her imagination was running a little wild. Terry's explanation for the theft certainly seemed more plausible than hers.

"It's probable," he corrected as he climbed into the Jeep and motioned for Allison to do the same. "Let's discuss it on the way home."

When she was settled, he gunned the engine and pulled forward. "The hard part, is remembering how we got here in the first place."

"The directions were in the notebook," Allison said, surveying the street. "I remember we turned at that small leather-goods kiosk."

"Yep." Terry cut the wheel, and the Jeep eased onto a crowded street.

He drove slowly, keeping alert for familiar landmarks. The Jeep wound through the maze of streets.

"There's the police station," Allison said at last, pointing to a building up the road.

"Yep." Terry replied, but he seemed distracted.

Allison turned to him and noticed his eyes glued to the rearview mirror.

"What are you watching?" she asked, turning in her seat.

"Don't turn around," he commanded, and she faced forward. "I think we're being followed. A little red two-door. It pulled out behind us just about the time we left Mrs. Montoya's."

He continued to inch the Jeep forward through the throngs of people and vehicles that crowded the narrow street.

"Watch out," Allison called, and he jammed on the

brakes, screeching to a halt just short of an elderly man crossing the road with a cane.

Terry exhaled loudly. "Whew! I almost caused an accident."

"Are we still being followed?" Allison asked, her voice tense, as the man shuffled onto the sidewalk.

Terry's eyes darted to the rearview. "Still there. Just one person in the car. The driver."

The police-headquarters building drifted past as the Jeep crept forward.

"I'm going to find out for sure," Terry said at last, slowing to nearly a stop to allow a procession of pedestrians to cross the street. Suddenly he stomped on the accelerator, and the Jeep lurched forward.

He cut the wheel hard to the left, and they leaped into the cramped alleyway they had used on the detour during their trip to the Montoyas'.

The Jeep accelerated quickly through the short stretch. Allison held her breath with fear. The walls of the buildings were close enough to touch. The mirrors mounted on the Jeep nearly grazed the red brick.

Terry handled the Jeep with quiet assurance. He jammed on the brakes as it neared the end of the alley and leaned on the horn as they exited onto the road.

"Look out!" Allison screamed.

A minitruck filled to overflowing with empty wooden packing crates appeared from out of nowhere, apparently headed for a detour through the alley.

Terry spun the wheel and dodged the truck, amid the wild honking of the horn and angry gesticulations of the other driver.

"That was close," Allison said with relief when the Jeep finally came to a halt.

"Too close," Terry said. He was gripping the wheel tightly, Allison noticed. "But it worked out great." He turned in his seat and watched the truck.

Allison followed his eyes. The minitruck inched slowly along the alley, its driver apparently attempting to balance the ungainly load by driving slowly. The truck completely blocked the roadway.

"If we were being followed," he said, "we've got a perfect chance to escape right now. Nothing will be able to move through the alley until that truck clears the other side. And by the looks of things, that's going to be a while."

Chapter Six

*T*he desert seemed to crawl past Allison's window with all the speed of an aged tortoise. She was in a hurry to get home but faced a ride of at least another four hours before she could expect to see her front door in Mesa.

Terry stared at the road stretching out ahead, straight for miles, shimmering in the desert heat.

"A penny for your thoughts," Allison said.

He smiled. "I think you know what's on my mind."

"Tell me, then," she chided. She didn't want to be the first to mention it.

"The Evil One. I was ready to dismiss the entire story of the Confederate gold as a hoax until that car started to follow us."

Allison felt a small surge of victory. "You just needed a little proof."

He laughed shortly. "I'm a Taurus. You know, the big, plodding bull. I like to look before I leap."

"I'm too impulsive," Allison said. "But I'm an Aries—we're supposed to be that way." She smiled to herself. She didn't put any stock in astrology but enjoyed reading her horoscope daily. Still, she was always vaguely pleased when her daily forecast seemed to match events in her life.

"Supposing the Evil One really does exist," Terry said. "How did he know that we would be showing up at Mrs. Montoya's house today?"

She mulled his question for a moment. "Maybe he simply staked her house out."

Terry shook his head. "I don't think so. Mrs. Montoya is an old woman and not likely to be out much. I doubt whether the Evil One would expect her to lead him on another expedition into the desert."

"But he could have been waiting for any visitors she might have had," Allison countered. "Like us."

"True, but how could he know when someone would show up? He couldn't simply wait and watch twenty-four hours a day."

Suddenly an idea occurred to Allison. "Wait a minute," she said, gathering her thoughts. "What if the man I saw that day out in the desert was the Evil One?"

Terry was silent, apparently considering her idea. "It's a possibility. Though I didn't see anyone."

Allison grew impatient. "Well, I did. Now, assuming there was a person out there . . . ."

"Okay," Terry assented, "someone was out there."

"Suppose it was the Evil One. He was obviously tracking Mr. Montoya, hoping to be led to the gold."

"Then why would Esteban claim that the Evil One had killed him? It seems as though keeping Esteban alive would have been his first priority, to lead him to the gold. But we know he didn't do that, because if he had, the Evil One would have claimed the gold and wouldn't be following us right now."

Allison mulled this over for a few minutes.

"Mr. Montoya suspected that his son had been murdered," she said at last. "Somehow he detected the man on his trail and decided to stop searching for the gold, realizing that he was in danger. But the Evil One cornered him and took his water. Maybe he promised more if Mr. Montoya led him to the treasure."

Allison watched the desert through the windshield. It was only a theory, of course, but it accounted for the facts of the case.

Terry nodded. "But Mr. Montoya wouldn't cooperate. Maybe he thought he could escape." He nodded again. "It certainly ties up all the loose ends."

Allison bit her lip. She suddenly realized that her theory held a gaping hole. "But why didn't the Evil One attack us when he saw us discover the old man?"

Terry ran his hands loosely over the steering wheel as he contemplated Allison's question. "It could be that he was reluctant to interfere because we outnumbered him. Or maybe he thought Mr. Montoya had died before we discovered him. After all, we didn't spend much time with the old man, and when we left, we left alone. Anyone watching would naturally assume that we had discovered a body. The Evil One wouldn't have risked an attack under those circumstances. He could make the old man's killing look like death by exposure, but it would have been difficult to mask two additional murders."

Allison nodded. "That's true."

"But that doesn't explain how the Evil One could

have known about our visit to Mrs. Montoya today," he added.

"I think I can explain that," Allison said. "He could easily have followed us back to your Jeep that day. He probably had a car of his own parked somewhere in the vicinity. When we left for the police station, he returned to his car and followed us. There's only one police station in Kingman, and we were there for quite a while filling out forms. It would have been an easy matter for him to locate your Jeep in the parking lot. He followed you home from there."

Terry whistled softly. "So he must have been watching me for the past couple of days to see where I went."

Allison considered the implications. "He knows that we visited Mrs. Montoya today."

"He suspects that we know something," Terry added. "But he doesn't know how much."

They drove a while longer, each lost in thought.

"Just a minute," Terry said. "Doesn't it seem strange to you that the Evil One would stake out my house? He could have no way of being certain that we had learned anything from the old man."

Allison agreed with a nod of her head.

"And for all he knows, we traveled to Nogales today to pay our respects to Mrs. Montoya."

"With possibly millions of dollars in gold at stake, don't you think that he would be willing to spend a few hours watching two strangers who had suddenly appeared from nowhere?" she asked.

Terry was quiet for a moment; then a smile spread across his face. "You're good; I have to admit it."

His tone puzzled Allison. "What do you mean?" she asked.

"I mean you're impulsive. You're an Aries. Here you are, jumping to a bunch of conclusions, and we're not even sure of the facts yet."

"How can you say that?" she asked. "The evidence certainly points to someone following us. How else can you explain that car in Nogales?"

"A shortcut," he said.

"What do you mean?"

"I mean, we took that alley as a shortcut, to avoid the crowds in downtown. The driver of that car was probably doing the same thing. And let's face facts—anyone setting out from Mrs. Montoya's neighborhood and heading for downtown Nogales would probably follow the same route we drove."

Allison couldn't dispute Terry's reasoning, but circumstances seemed to indicate some truth to the story of the Confederate gold. "If it was only the car, I would go along with you," she said, giving voice to her thoughts. "But with everything else that's happened, I think we should consider the possibility that Mrs. Montoya is telling the truth."

"All right," he agreed. "We'll consider it." He stomped on the gas pedal and passed a slow-moving semi.

Allison watched Terry as he drove. The afternoon sun filtering through the windshield danced off his wavy blond hair and highlighted his strong nose and firm jaw. He was the picture of a pioneer, Allison thought. Rugged, strong, and handsome.

"Is there any way you would be able to check out

that story about the Confederate rebels in Arizona?" he asked her suddenly. "Verifying that would at least lend some credibility to the legend of the lost gold."

"I've had some experience in the research department," Allison replied wryly. She was, in fact, intimately familiar with the Phoenix City Library and often spent entire days there tracking down information for her stories. "I was planning on doing some investigation on this thing, anyway."

"Oh, you were, were you?" Terry glanced her way and smiled. "I think I'd like to be kept informed about this."

"But I didn't think you believed Mrs. Montoya's story," she teased.

"That doesn't mean I'm not interested."

"Just for the sake of history, I suppose."

"Exactly." Terry smiled. "And I could use the money, too, just in case the story pans out." He pretended to laugh and poked Allison in the ribs. "Get it? Pans out? That's an old gold prospector's joke."

Allison tried to dodge Terry's hand but missed. "Cut it out," she said playfully, pushing it away. "I guess prospectors don't have much of a sense of humor."

"No sense of humor? How can you say that? I've read every joke book ever written."

"That may be your problem."

"You're just mad because you didn't think of it," he said good-naturedly.

"You have a way of seeing right through me, don't you, Braun?" she chided with a smile.

"You're a writer," he said. "Write me a joke book."

She considered the proposition. "I just might. At least then I could laugh at your jokes."

Terry shrugged and pulled past a tanker truck. They continued to banter back and forth for several minutes. Allison felt herself relaxing in the lighthearted atmosphere.

Sitting beside him in the Jeep, she saw a thoughtful, witty man. And she could hardly escape noticing his muscular arms as he held the steering wheel. She was suddenly finding it difficult to keep her eyes off him. She forced herself to look at the scenery through her window. She didn't want to appear to be a giddy high-school girl enamored with her first date.

The desert south of Tucson was green as far as deserts go. The Sonoran Desert held a wide variety of plant life. Mesquite and paloverde sprouted from the baked desert floor, and everywhere giant saguaro cacti towered over the landscape, their enormous, dull-green arms, covered with sharp needles, reaching toward the blue Arizona sky.

Terry coughed softly to himself, and Allison glanced quickly in his direction. He stared intently down the road. She wondered what he was thinking about. She turned back to the desert.

She found herself attracted to Terry, but a familiar fear gnawed at her. She closed her eyes and tried to sort out her emotions. Her whole life, it seemed, had been governed by her own fear of involvement.

Not that she had never dated men. She smiled as she recalled her days in college. Todd Garrigan. His face invariably popped into her mind whenever she thought of her college days. They had spent months together, but Allison realized she had never really known him. After graduation Todd had moved to southern California to take a job with an aeronautics firm, and Allison had remained in Mesa, working at a local newspaper.

The Jeep jostled over a rough patch on the road. "Ride 'em cowboy," Terry said, bouncing in his seat.

Allison watched him, and he smiled at her.

Oh, it's hopeless, she thought as she returned his smile. She turned her gaze back to the desert. It was an awful feeling to be attracted to a man but afraid to show it.

A small collection of mobile homes shimmering whitely in the desert on the outskirts of Tucson caught her eye, and she found herself thinking of her mother.

Emily Ames had married late in life. She had confessed to her daughter once that she had waited so long because she had wanted to be certain that the man she married was the right man. And when she had finally married, at the age of thirty-five, she had been sure that she had found just such a man.

Allison's father had left home when she was just an infant. He had told her mother that he didn't know how to raise children and had left. He had walked out the door, Allison imagined, like a man on his way to the corner grocer to pick up a quart of milk. He never returned.

Emily Ames had endured her heartache silently. Even at the very end, lying in the hospital bed, dying of cancer, she had never uttered a bitter word about the man who had abandoned them. His leaving, though, had had a profound effect on their lives.

Allison remembered growing up in a mobile home,

just like the ones the Jeep was now passing. She remembered her mother working at the diner all day and doing piecework for a local factory at night.

She remembered spending Christmas alone with her mother, while silently praying for a father, and she remembered used toys under the tree and canned donations on the table.

She remembered too much, she thought as the mobile homes passed her window. But mostly she remembered that her father had abandoned her mother and left her heartbroken, with a baby to raise.

Allison tried to erase the unpleasant memories from her mind, but she knew it would be impossible. Those memories were as much a part of her as her hair or her eyes. They couldn't be removed, and they would never be forgotten.

Glancing toward Terry, she felt a longing and a yearning, but over it all was the fear, like a heavy black blanket, of giving her heart to a man, only to have it crushed. Only to be abandoned.

Terry's eyes were glued to the rearview mirror. Allison noticed that the Jeep was slowing. "Is something wrong?" she asked, attempting conversation, hoping to derail the melancholy feeling that had overtaken her.

"Just checking something," he said, his eyes shifting from the mirror to the roadway, then back again to the mirror.

Allison watched the speedometer needle dip. Terry wasn't braking, but he had removed his foot from the gas pedal, and the Jeep was slowly coasting to a stop. The needle swung backward over the face of the speedometer.

"Why are you stopping?" she asked, puzzled by his behavior.

"Just a minute." He applied his foot to the accelerator, and the Jeep's speed leveled off at forty miles per hour. "I think we're being followed."

Allison twisted in her seat, alarmed. Down the road in the distance, she could just make out the red speck of a car through the shimmering heat on the interstate.

"When I slow down, he slows down," Terry said. He pressed the gas pedal, and the Jeep sped forward.

Allison continued to watch the car.

"He'll speed up to keep even with us," Terry predicted. "He'll stay just that far away from us. Just to where he can maintain a tail and still be hard to spot."

The distance between the Jeep and the car remained constant. Allison asked, "How long has he been back there?"

"I first spotted him over half an hour ago. The car that followed us into that alley in Nogales was red, remember?"

She nodded.

"I've been varying my speed slightly up and down ever since I noticed him, but he's never overtaken us. He's never disappeared from my rearview, either."

Allison's heart was beating heavily. "The Evil One?" she asked.

"It's someone," was all he would say.

Suddenly Allison was filled with fear. Terry had been willing to dismiss talk of the Evil One earlier, but now he seemed to think it possible that they were being followed.

The interstate was nearly devoid of cars. Allison's

imagination ran wild. What if they were overtaken and run off the road? "I'm scared," she said.

Terry looked at her and winked reassuringly. "I don't think you have anything to worry about. If he is following us, it isn't to do us any harm, but to find out where we're going." He glanced again into the rearview. "In any event," he said, "we're almost to Tucson. I'm pretty familiar with the area. We'll stop in for dinner and see if we can lose him on some back streets."

Allison watched the following car through the rear window. Terry pressed the accelerator to the floor, and the Jeep leaped forward. The red car, she noticed, maintained the interval.

Chapter Seven

"**I** didn't think that university professors really worked," Allison said, standing on the threshold of Terry's office, smiling as she watched him fumble through a sheaf of papers.

"Allison," he exclaimed, obviously surprised and pleased at her unannounced visit. "What brings you around this fine day?" He continued flipping through the papers.

"Just a little information I thought you might be interested in," she responded, stepping into the office and taking a seat on a gray metal folding chair that was positioned against the wall.

"Come in. How are you?" He tossed the papers into a ragged pile in the center of his desk and faced her. "I'm sorry," he said, "but I've lost a manpower report somewhere, and you know how it is. The university has its bureaucracy just like anyplace else."

She eyed the tiny office. The walls were adorned with every type of map she could imagine, illustrating, she guessed, every country on the face of the earth and some, she thought wryly, that hadn't yet been discovered.

Steel utility shelves, the type usually reserved for storing tools in garages, lined the walls and were crammed to overflowing with a variety of books. Most dealt with geology, though Allison also noted several works of fiction among the collection.

"So this is your home away from home?" she asked, standing up to examine a fist-sized rock atop Terry's desk.

"No," he said. "*This* is my home. The other place, where I sleep, *that's* my home away from home."

She turned the rock in her hand. It had been broken in two, and the center was hollow and lined with crystals.

"It's a geode," he explained, noting her interest. "The crystals are formed by gases trapped inside the rock. I found that one on the Colorado River, just south of Hoover Dam." He watched her looking at the rock. "Just tapped it with my pick and busted it open. Usually you try to save both halves of the stone, so you can put the top and bottom together." He shrugged. "I lost the top somewhere along the line.

"When I was a kid," he continued, "I used to like to crack walnuts open and very carefully take out the insides. Then I'd glue them back together and replace them in the nut dish. I always thought that people would be really puzzled when they cracked the nuts and found nothing inside."

"That old Terry Braun humor again," Allison said. She nodded at the geode. "The crystals in that look a little dusty."

"Leave it to you to notice." Terry leaned forward in his seat and hefted the stone. He stared into the hollow at the crystals. "I had a guy from the physics department in here one day talking about volcanoes, and he lit up a cigar." He returned the geode to his desk and gestured with both hands. "A big cigar. You know, a stogey." He held his hands about a foot apart to emphasize what he was saying. "He lit up, filled my office with smoke, and used the geode as an ashtray."

"You've got to be kidding," she said, smiling with disbelief.

"I couldn't believe it myself. And I was sitting here watching it."

"What did you do?"

He twisted his lip and shrugged. "I was polite about it. I offered him an ashtray and told him that he had just ruined a priceless geode." He laughed at the memory. "Anyway," he said, leaning forward, "you said you have some information. It's about the gold, I suspect."

"That's right."

He twisted in his seat and crossed his legs. "Well"— he gestured with his hands, looking up at Allison, who was still standing before his desk—"let's have it."

"It will cost you. One lunch."

He chuckled. "That's one way to guarantee a date. Bribery."

"Then we have a deal?" she asked slyly, knowing he would agree.

He laughed good-naturedly. "We have a deal," he said with a nod. Then he uncrossed his legs and lifted the stack of papers from his desk. "But first I have a manpower report to locate. Believe it or not, university professors really do work.''

Allison dropped into the metal folding chair. "I'll wait. It will just make me hungrier."

"Uh-oh." Terry sighed. "I'd better find that report soon."

The Wagontrain was a small burger restaurant close to the university campus. Sawdust was scattered on the floor, and the tables, which were simply enormous wooden spools that had once been used to transport electrical cable, were covered with red plaid tablecloths.

The lunch-hour crunch was in high gear, and faculty and students crowded the tiny establishment. "Over here," Terry beckoned, leading Allison to a table for two that was just being vacated.

"Good eyes," she said, settling into her seat.

"Comes from years of experience."

A busboy appeared, cleared the table of dirty dishes, and set fresh place settings.

"So what's the news?" Terry asked.

"Well, it probably won't make headlines," Allison said, looking at her menu, "but I'm starving."

"I meant the news about the gold."

She grinned. "I know," she teased. "But that doesn't change that fact that I'm famished." She eyed the menu. "I don't think I'll be able to talk about what I discovered, until I order the most expensive thing on the menu."

Terry laughed and sipped his water. "I should have known. It had better be good news."

She allowed herself a cryptic smile. Maybe it was, maybe it wasn't.

A waitress dressed in tight blue jeans and a snug T-shirt came to take their order. Her long dark hair flowed over her shoulders, and her eyes, which were locked onto Terry, were heavily made up. Her name tag said Pam. She was obviously a college student. She jotted their order onto her pad, not once taking her eyes from Terry, and wandered off.

"I'm surprised," Terry commented. "You didn't get the most expensive meal."

"I thought I would give you a break," she said, fighting a tug of jealousy as she watched Pam turn into the kitchen.

"I appreciate that. So what did you find out?"

"First, I want to know if you've seen anything more of that red car." Even though they hadn't been followed upon leaving Tucson, the incident still weighed on her mind.

Terry shook his head. "No. I think we were just overreacting to everything we'd heard about the Evil One and the gold." He smoothed his napkin. "After all, there *is* only one road leading from Nogales to Tucson. Anyone traveling north would naturally use it."

"But why wouldn't he pass us?" she asked, doubting Terry's explanation.

"Hard to say," he replied frankly. "But he was nowhere in sight when we left Tucson, and that's all that matters."

"It just seems like too much of a coincidence," she argued. "The same person who pulled out behind us just down the street from Mrs. Montoya's house in Nogales ends up shadowing us along the freeway to Tucson. Remember Pablo Ramirez lives just across the street from the Montoyas. He could have seen us pull out and decided to follow us."

"We don't know for a fact that the red car in Nogales and the red car on the freeway were the same car," he countered. "Sometimes it seems as though every other car on the road is red. It was probably just someone driving from Nogales to Tucson."

"Probably?" she asked, seizing his doubt.

"All right," he confessed. "There is a lot of coincidence. But I honestly think that that's all it is—coincidence. Besides, if we follow your theory, the Evil One has already discovered where I live. He would have no need to follow us from Nogales."

"Yes, he would," she countered. "He couldn't know what Mrs. Montoya told us. He had to follow us on the chance that we might lead him to the gold."

Pam arrived with their food. Without taking her eyes from Terry, she set a large plate before Allison. "The Wagontrain burger," she said. She winked at Terry. "And the All-American cheeseburger," she said, setting Terry's plate down with entirely too much flourish. "Will there be anything else?" she asked with a smile.

Allison felt a faint stirring of jealousy. *Slow down,* she told herself. *Terry is a regular here. He has his own life.* Besides, she had no claim on him. Still, Pam's attentions raised her defenses.

"I think we're just about set," Terry was saying, a smile on his face.

"Holler if you need me," Pam said. She cast a short glance at Allison and left.

"Are you ever going to tell me what you found out about the gold?" Terry asked.

His question diverted Allison's thoughts from the waitress to the trip she had made to the Phoenix City Library earlier that morning.

"Did you find the map?" he asked. His voice held a slightly joking tone.

She poured some ketchup on her hamburger. She enjoyed the suspense she was creating. Despite his protestations to the contrary, it was obvious that Terry was interested in the story of the lost Confederate gold.

"I wasn't looking for the map," she said after a pause. "Besides, there are thousands of books. I don't know how anyone could be expected to find anything hidden there. We wouldn't even know where to begin looking."

"I didn't think you'd really been searching for the map," he said, but Allison thought she noticed the subtlest hint of disappointment in his voice. "It's always nice to dream, though."

"I did do some research on Mrs. Montoya's story, however." She took a bite of her hamburger.

"And?"

She nodded her head. "It's good."

"The news?"

"No, the hamburger." She laughed at her joke and smiled at Terry, who wore an exasperated expression.

"Okay," he said. "Whose sense of humor needs improvement now?"

She sipped her drink. "I wasn't able to find much information," she admitted, "but considering the top-secret nature of the gold shipment, I don't think that's too surprising."

"But you did find something?"

"Well, I did most of my searching through old records of lost treasures and abandoned mines. There are literally hundreds in the state of Arizona. The lost Confederate gold isn't exactly one of the better-known treasures."

"But it is mentioned somewhere?" His voice was tinged with excitement.

"I only found one mention of it. Just a short paragraph in a passage from a pamphlet published by the State Mining Commission in 1926. It didn't give any information, really. It just made mention of the legend." She reached down to her feet, brought up her purse, and extracted a sheet of paper. "I made a copy of the page, and circled the passage." She handed the paper to Terry.

He read it quickly. "You're right. This isn't very encouraging."

"It's better than nothing. At least we know that the story wasn't simply concocted by Esteban Montoya."

Terry looked thoughtful. "You're right. In a way, I guess, this tiny little passage could even make Montoya's claim more believable. I mean, if this legend is that obscure, I doubt whether he could have read anything about it prior to making his claims."

"Exactly," she agreed. She had had the same thought. "This article makes me believe Mrs. Montoya's story all the more."

"But just a minute," he interrupted, munching on a French fry. "I did a little investigating on my own this morning."

Allison raised an inquiring eyebrow.

"I talked to a friend of mine, Alex, in the history department. He said it was ridiculous to imagine the English sending a shipment of gold to a band of Confederate rebels, even if they had gone along with the plan to move the Civil War into Arizona—which, by the way, he says is ludicrous as well."

Terry took a bite of his hamburger. Allison was anxious to hear what he had to say but resisted the urge to prompt him. He was, she realized, using the same dramatic techniques on her that she had been using on him.

"Anyway," he finally said, "Alex said that gold would hardly have helped the rebels. They needed weapons, ammunition, and supplies, and the Union, which was the only supplier of such things when the war was finally winding down, wasn't in the business of making sales to the Confederates. Also, gold wouldn't have been much use in bribing the Indians. The Apaches didn't have any use for money. Weapons would have made a much better bargaining tool."

Allison sighed. "So he doesn't think the legend of the lost Confederate gold is for real?"

"No, but that shouldn't be much of a surprise. If more people took the legend seriously, the gold would probably have been discovered by now."

"Or at least the legend could have been proved a hoax," she suggested.

"Who's doubting the story now? Anyway, legends have a way of growing over time. For all we know, the Confederate 'gold' may be no more than a photo of Jefferson Davis in a gilt frame."

She smiled. He was right. Her initial enthusiasm

about the legend had waned in the light of her disappointing morning at the library. Alex's gloomy pronouncements had only served to further dampen her mood. She had hoped for something that would prove the legend either true or false. Instead, she was right back where she had begun. "I just don't know what to believe," she said.

"I think we should head up to Kingman for another look around. We never did get around to finding your turquoise, remember?"

"I was meaning to talk to you about that," she said with a grin. "I still want to finish that article."

"We can get up there any time you want to go."

"Would Friday be all right?"

He laughed. "Well, not quite *any* time. I have a couple of classes to teach on Friday morning. Is Friday night good?"

"I don't think we'll find much turquoise by the light of the moon," she said, secretly thrilled with the idea of a midnight stroll through the desert with him.

"We will if it's full," he told her. "Or, at least I'm sure we'll find something."

"We'll just wait until Saturday morning."

"Nine o'clock?"

"That would be fine." But Allison couldn't help but wonder what sort of things she might have found if she had taken him up on his offer to go searching by moonlight.

Chapter Eight

*I*t seemed to Allison as though Saturday would never arrive. Though she occupied herself by writing a number of articles she had been delaying, her thoughts were constantly revolving around Terry, Mrs. Montoya, and the Confederate gold.

She finished an article for a consumer magazine, detailing options available when purchasing a swimming pool, and wrote a vacation piece for a mass-circulation leisure publication.

She had attempted to work on her novel but had found it nearly impossible to concentrate on it with the events of the past week weighing on her mind.

Thoughts of Terry continually interrupted her work. Somehow his brief absence from her life, coupled with the anticipation of the good things that would transpire on their next meeting, combined to create a longing in Allison.

She attempted to dismiss her newfound infatuation by convincing herself that she was really only interested in the Confederate gold, but her rationalizations could not dissuade her from admitting the truth to herself.

Terry's friendliness and sense of humor were magnetic. He had about him a charisma that seemed to draw Allison toward him. And his physique was incredible. She was attracted to him as she had never before been attracted to a man.

The ride to the area where they had discovered Mr. Montoya took almost four hours. As Terry's Jeep raced northward toward Kingman, he and Allison discussed the day's plans.

"Keep in mind," he said, "that our primary purpose for this trip is to finish up that piece you were doing on turquoise."

"Who are you trying to kid?" she teased. In light of the legend of the lost gold, she had all but forgotten about her hunt for turquoise.

"Of course," he continued, "we'll be able to wrap that up in no time. Then we'll get to the important business of gold hunting."

The road twisted through high desert country, peppered with Joshua trees, blue paloverde, and velvet mesquite. The relatively high amount of rainfall in this area supported a wide variety of plant life that even in the summer cast a thin veil of green over the brown earth.

"I think that this is the most beautiful country in the world," she said, admiring the constantly changing mosaic of terrain and vegetation.

The Jeep crested a hill. "Just look at the view," Terry commented.

"You can see for miles," she exclaimed. A rugged valley stretched out below them. In contrast to the green of the high desert, the valley appeared to be stark and lifeless. A line of jagged gray mountains ripped the horizon far in the distance. The sun blazed in a cloudless sky, bathing the valley with heat.

Terry nodded his head toward the valley. "Welcome to the Mojave Desert."

The pair made good time descending from the high desert into the low country. The road wound down through the hills like a snake, curving left, then right, then left again, never straight for more than a passing moment, and surrounded on both sides by hills of gray dirt through which the road had been cut.

At last the highway straightened and the desert flattened. They were traveling along the desert floor now. Heat shimmered off the blacktop in waves, and the roadway dissolved to a point miles ahead in the distance. There seemed to be no other cars on the road.

Allison noticed that Terry was continually checking his rearview mirror.

"Are we being followed?" she asked, suddenly alarmed.

He laughed self-consciously. "Caught me peeking," he said. He glanced at her. "Nothing behind us that I can see."

"I thought you were willing to dismiss that red car as coincidence," she commented, turning to gaze back along the highway. All she saw were the white stripes on the road appearing, then disappearing, in a seemingly endless progression.

"It probably was," he said. "But I'm not going to bet everything on it." He turned quickly in his seat and shrugged toward the cargo compartment. "Grab that," he told her, nodding at a long brown nylon case. A pair of tan carrying handles were stitched to the fabric about halfway up its length.

She pulled the case forward and unzipped it.

"It's a .30-.30," he explained. "My deer rifle. A little bit of insurance, just in case."

She pulled the weapon from the case and examined it. The barrel was long and black. The stock was dark walnut and was engraved with a series of diamonds. The butt was of matching wood and was also decorated with diamonds. A thick rubber heel extended from the butt, some type of shoulder pad, she reasoned.

"I've never much cared for guns," she said.

"Why's that?" he asked. Allison noticed no defensive tones, just curiosity.

She shrugged. "Honestly, I've just never been interested in them. I've never given them any thought, I suppose. I don't see much need for them."

"I've always loved guns," Terry said. "I've had them ever since I was a little boy. First a BB gun, then a .22, a shotgun, some pistols. I guess I've used just about all types of guns."

"Do you really hunt deer?" she asked, hoping he would say no.

"I've gone a couple of times for mule deer out in the Kaibab Range, but I've never bagged anything."

"You wouldn't really shoot one, would you?"

"Why wouldn't I?"

"They just seem so graceful and proud, living out there in the wild, I don't see how you could do such a thing."

Terry nodded. "That's fair. I guess when you're sitting at home in the comfort of your living room, looking at pictures of animals in the wild, it's easy to consider hunting as inhumane." He looked over at her. "I could argue that the State Department of Fish and Game has set quotas for deer kills based on the fact that herds need to be cut back annually to prevent widespread starvation, but that wouldn't really answer your question.

"There's a kind of excitement in the hunt. Man against nature. When you've spent days stalking a buck and you finally get him in your sights, your adrenaline takes charge. The buck is no longer simply a deer; it is your quarry. Any stray noise will send him charging, and your chance will be lost. Any stray whiff of your scent, and he'll bolt. It really is a challenge. And there's something in me that likes to win."

"But I still don't see how you could actually kill a living, breathing deer," Allison said. "Couldn't you simply take a photograph to prove how close you came?"

"I suppose I could, but it wouldn't be the same."

"You mean, it wouldn't prove that you had actually conquered nature."

"I never said I wanted to conquer nature," he pointed out. "Only that I enjoyed the chase. As a matter of fact, though I've had several opportunities, I've never killed a deer. I always miss the crucial shot for some reason."

"It's your conscience pulling the trigger. You're too nice a guy to kill a deer."

He laughed. "I like you too."

Allison gazed at him thoughtfully, a slight smile tugging at the corner of her lips.

Terry, noticing her attention, turned to her and

smiled. He placed his hand at the base of her neck and tousled her hair. "I'm glad we got together again," he said, his hand sliding around her shoulder.

"Me too."

He checked the rearview one more time. "Still an empty road. It looks like we're all alone out here. Just you and me."

"Um-hmmm." She closed her eyes and let her head rest back against his arm.

They lapsed into an intimate silence, lost in their thoughts of each other as the scenery sped by.

The desert was as hot and dry as it had been the day they had discovered the dying Mr. Montoya. It seemed impossible to Allison that only one week had passed. She and Terry neared the location quietly, each recalling the events of that day.

"This is the place," he remarked as they approached the stone-littered bank of the draw where they had discovered Mr. Montoya's crumpled form. Patches of sweat spread from under the rifle sling strapped to Terry's shoulder.

Allison stared mutely at the hostile ground. It didn't seem possible that a man could die here one day, and one week later not a trace would remain of his passing.

"Let's move on," Terry said.

Without another word, they continued up the dry wash bed.

After a short hike Terry stopped and indicated the ground of the wash. "We're here. Turquoise pretty much lies on the surface around this place."

Allison scanned the packed sand of the wash bed. She

was hot and thirsty, and perspiration streaked her face. The canvas strap of the canteen, slung over her shoulder, bit into her neck. She pulled it free and took a drink. "I don't know exactly what I'm looking for," she admitted.

"The turquoise in this area is greener than the stuff found around Bisbee," he said, mentioning the famous boomtown in central Arizona. "The Bisbee blue brings a higher price, but that's because it's more difficult to find. Your readers will appreciate this location because the stones are pretty much on the surface."

She kicked some rocks near her feet. "So what do we look for?"

"The stone will be a medium green in color, but that's only after cutting and polishing. What we're going to find here will be dusty and dirty; the color will be partially obscured, but the green will be there. All it takes is a little patience and a careful eye."

Allison skirted the edges of the wash slowly, her eyes intent on the ground. Terry followed behind.

"Here we are," he called. She turned to see him on one knee, handling a small stone. He glanced up at her and tossed the rock. "There you go."

Allison caught the turquoise and studied it.

Terry appeared at her side. He licked his thumb and rubbed it across the rock. The faint green of the stone took on a lustrous quality.

"See the matrix?" he asked, indicating the tiny brown veins that crisscrossed the stone. "Bisbee blue has a deeper color, but Mineral Park turquoise has a much nicer matrix."

Allison turned the stone in her hand to compare the

colors of the cleaned rock with the hue of the stone as it was found in the wash. "The dirty side looks hazy," she noted. "Like algae in a mud pond."

"That's one way of describing it. These stones are green because they contain so much copper. We're pretty close to the Mineral Park Copper Mines, as a matter of fact." He indicated a direction with a vague nod of his head. "Turquoise has always been pretty much a byproduct of the copper-mining operations around here. A lucrative byproduct, however."

He glanced at the ground, shifting his gaze back and forth, looking for more turquoise.

"There's one," she exclaimed, spotting another piece of telltale green stone. She bent and scooped it up.

"Nice piece." Terry nodded, eyeing the sample as Allison cleaned it with a wetted forefinger. "It's easy, isn't it, once you know what you're looking for?"

"This is fun," she said joyfully, excited that she had actually discovered a semiprecious stone.

"Back in the old days," Terry told her, "a subcontractor used to work the Mineral Park Copper Mine, doing nothing but collecting turquoise that was uncovered in the copper-mining operation. Relatively speaking, this area is littered with turquoise. Your readers should have a field day out here."

Allison pocketed the stone she had discovered, and Terry handed her the one he had found. "Want to look for some more?" he asked.

"Sure. I want to find enough to make a bracelet."

"That should be easy." He moved up the wash, his eyes locked on the ground. Suddenly he bent low and picked a piece from the ground. "Each of these stones could be cut into several small stones, then polished and placed in a bracelet."

"How many of them do you think we'll need?" she asked.

"Four or five stones should be enough."

"Is that all?" She felt slightly disappointed. She enjoyed the hunt almost as much as the reward of finding the stones.

"I'm afraid so. Why? Did you want to bring home more?"

"I wanted a sack full," she confessed. She spotted a piece of turquoise and snatched it up.

He chuckled. "You seem to be enjoying this." He crossed the short distance separating them. "The chase is fun," he said, circling his arms around her, "but the capture is better."

She stared longingly into his clear blue eyes and saw only honesty and sincerity.

He leaned forward and kissed her gently.

Allison's hands roamed up the sides of his chest, feeling the ripples of muscles. "I think you caught me," she said quietly.

"Maybe it's the other way around," he told her, tilting his face to hers.

She was flooded with excitement as their lips met for a second time.

He hugged her tightly to his body. She could feel his warmth through his shirt.

The sweet smell of the desert floated on the air. His hands pressed into her back, pulling her closer.

The moment defied description. It seemed to last forever, while taking no time at all. Too quickly, he straightened and said, "I think we have other business to look into."

The look in his eyes hinted at the nature of the business he wanted to investigate. Standing so close to him, she wondered if she would have the strength to resist. She took a deep breath. *Slow down,* she told herself. *True love requires time.*

She smiled and countered his advance by saying, "That other business is gold, as I recall." She played absently with a button on his shirt.

"What other business did you think I had in mind?" he asked with a grin and a chuckle. He eyed her closely, then stepped away and studied the ground. "Last one," he said, leaning over for a final turquoise stone. He handed it to Allison, who quickly pocketed it.

He inhaled deeply and exhaled quickly, as though trying to regain his composure. "Let's try to get the lay of the land," he suggested. "I've been out here before, but never looking for a cache of lost gold. I want to get a feel for this place." He pointed to a nearby hill. "That looks like the highest point around. We'll be able to get a good view from the top."

Allison groaned silently to herself. Though she was interested in solving the mystery of the Confederate gold, she had no desire to go mountain climbing in this heat.

Apparently reading her expression, Terry promised, "Don't worry, we'll take it easy."

They eased slowly up the side of the hill, pausing twice for water and rest. When they finally reached the top, they commanded a view of a large portion of the valley.

To the north, the terrain was pocked by a series of ridges. A magnificent purple-hued spire of rock poked from the desert floor on the east.

On the west, the flat plain of the Mojave broke into scarred, rutted earth. A flood plain, evidently. The ground had been gouged into an unending succession of dry wash beds.

A large mesa could be seen about one mile away to the southwest. Sheer gray cliffs led to the summit of the flat-topped mountain.

Allison's eyes roamed the desert between the dune where she stood and the mesa. It was uneven, dusty, and treacherously rocky.

Terry was silent for several seconds, surveying the landscape. "That's a lot of land," he said at last with a short laugh. "We can't even be certain that Esteban Montoya was in the vicinity of the gold when we discovered him."

"But Mrs. Montoya was certain that her husband knew where it was," Allison reminded him.

"Of course he knew. These old treasure hounds are always one step away from uncovering the money. I've noticed that they generally die poor."

She refused to become caught up in his cynicism. "Let's suppose that Esteban Montoya really had located the gold," she persisted. "How far could he have wandered once he discovered that he was being followed?"

Terry thought for a moment. "It's hard to say. It would have depended on the terrain. If he had been wandering through the mountains, he would have covered less ground than if he had been walking on the flat."

"I suppose you're right. But we can guesstimate his direction of travel, can't we? Using the articles of clothing we found along the trail as a type of pointer, showing us where he had come from."

"By the time he was stripping his clothes," Terry said, "he was already blinded by thirst and heat, so that wouldn't really provide us with any clues."

Allison scanned the hostile terrain. "There's only one way we'll ever have a chance of finding that gold," she said at last.

"You're right. We've got to find the map."

She nodded. "The one Mr. Montoya hid in the public library."

Chapter Nine

*T*he Phoenix City Library was situated on a long lawn of green grass on Central Avenue, just beyond the skyscrapers that bordered the business district. The three-story structure reflected contemporary Southwestern architecture. Its stucco walls were painted a light shade of pink, and the trim was finished in soft pastels. Arched windows lined the sides of the building, their lightly tinted glass glinting in the afternoon sun. A concrete walkway dividing the lawn into even halves stopped at heavily tinted automatic glass doors that opened into the building.

The doors slid open with a gentle whisper as Allison and Terry entered the air-conditioned comfort of the library.

"Here we are," she said, motioning with her hand.

Terry's eyes slowly roamed the interior. "You've got to be kidding. Talk about searching for a needle in a haystack."

"You mean you've never been here before?" she asked, noting his reaction.

"Don't sound so surprised. I do most of my research

93

at the university library." He continued to survey the library. "I visited here long ago. Very long ago. It was a lot smaller in those days. I guess the place has grown up since then."

Allison couldn't help but smile. "It's pretty big," she agreed.

From the spacious foyer, tastefully decorated with the paintings and artwork of local artists, she could see rows of books filling the cavernous first floor of the library. Banks of tables holding computer keyboards and CRTs lined the walls. These were the computerized card catalogs. Through the countless hours of research she had conducted there, Allison had practically memorized every inch of the library.

The first floor held the library's fiction collection, two spacious reading rooms, an information desk, and a book checkout area. The second floor contained nonfiction and reference materials, and the third floor held the library's periodical collection. In the basement could be found special reference materials, available for short-term use only.

"I've been thinking about where Esteban might have hidden the map," Allison said.

Terry crossed the white marble floor of the foyer, to the brown carpet that stretched across the fiction area. "Let me guess," he ventured, facing the lines of book-shelves. "You have over one hundred thousand ideas about where it might be."

"I'll excuse your tepid attempt at sarcasm," she said dryly. "As a matter of fact, I know this library like the back of my hand, and I think I know where we can begin our search."

"Begin?" he asked incredulously. "Begin our search? Look at this place. It's bigger than a barn. It's bigger than two barns. You don't begin a search here; you begin a lifetime undertaking."

"If you would stop complaining for a minute and listen to me, you'd find out that the job isn't nearly as enormous as it appears."

"That's good. Because it looks bigger than enormous."

She joined him on the carpet, and they crossed to the elevator on the far wall. Since Mrs. Montoya hadn't known the title of the book her husband had hidden the map in, Allison had attempted to logically deduce its location.

"I figured that since Esteban didn't speak English, he would have been working in the Spanish-language collection on the second floor," she told him, pushing a button with an arrow pointing upward.

"Hey, that's good," he said. "You ought to be a detective."

She smiled. "Like Sham Shpade, you mean?" she asked, affecting her best Bogart.

"That's pretty good," he joked. "Now do Bogart." He grabbed her about the waist and pulled her close to his side. "I don't think you'd make much money in the impersonation business."

She grinned and allowed herself to lean into him. His body was firm and muscular. "I'll just give it a little practice," she said.

He squeezed her. "A lot of practice."

The elevator doors slid open and they rode to the second floor.

They walked to the shelves holding the Spanish-language collection. "Nonfiction occupies this side," Allison explained, indicating several shelves laden with books, "and this side holds the fiction." She nodded to another collection of shelves.

"Well," Terry sighed, eyeing the hundreds of books, "that really narrows things down."

"Quit being such a gloomy Gus. Use your head. Esteban Montoya wanted revenge on the Evil One. He wanted to give away what the Evil One couldn't steal."

A look of genuine interest crossed Terry's face. "I can tell you have this all figured out."

"I have an idea or two."

"So do I," he said softly, placing his hands on her shoulders.

"The map," Allison said, enjoying Terry's attention but attempting to remain serious. "Remember the map?"

"You don't really believe that story, do you?" His voice was soft and close.

Her pleasure was replaced by a flash of anger. She pushed his hands from her body and stepped back. "Don't you?" she asked. "Or are you only here to play games?"

His face took on a pained expression. "I'm here because I want to be here," he said in an attempt to smooth over the situation. He stepped toward her.

"We're in a public library," she snapped, taking another step back and crossing her arms across her chest.

"What's this all about?" he asked, his voice edged with a hint of anger.

"How can you ask that? We've been working together on this Confederate gold mystery, and all the time you've obviously considered it just one big joke." Suddenly Allison remembered how often Terry had voiced doubts about the gold. "You've just been playing along." The anger rose in her voice.

She forced herself to remain calm, reminding herself that she was in a library. "I hope you got a good laugh watching me rummage for clues," she said tersely. "But I believe in Mrs. Montoya, and I'm not going to give up on finding the gold or discovering who murdered her husband and her son." She paused just long enough to fire a mean glance at Terry. "You can leave. I wouldn't want to bore you."

A slight smile appeared on his face. "You're not boring me."

Terry's demeanor caught Allison by surprise. She had expected anger, not a smile, no matter how tentative.

"You don't believe in the gold," she said. "I suppose that you've only played along this far because you wanted to see me make a fool of myself."

"You're right about one thing, at least. I have never completely believed the gold story. I think Esteban Montoya believed in it, though, and so did his son. And I think they died in the desert north of Kingman because they believed in it."

"I knew it," Allison muttered, her anger somewhat dissipated by Terry's frank admission.

"But you were wrong about the other thing," he continued, the smile again playing like a shadow on his face. "I never wanted to laugh at you."

"Then what did you want? To waste my time?"

"No," he said, and the smile spread over his face. "I wanted to be with you."

His candid confession took Allison completely by surprise. She felt like a deflated balloon. She was ashamed of her outburst and felt guilty for having assumed devious motives for his behavior.

She realized that she couldn't simply walk away from the matter, and she wanted to be certain she soothed Terry's feelings. There was, she realized, only one way to handle the situation, and that was with honesty.

"I'm sorry," she said sincerely. "I had no right to say the things I said."

He brushed her apology away with a smile and a wave of his hand. "Forget it."

"No. I'm really sorry." She searched his face for any hint of malice and found none. "Are you telling me the truth? You only came along to be with me?"

He smiled. "Isn't it reason enough?"

Allison's heart was racing. Terry was so close, and he seemed so sincere. "I want to be with you too," she said. She wanted to hold him and never let him go. Still, the faintest stirrings of unease rippled through her. Could she trust herself to him, or would he simply steal her heart, then leave her, as her father had left her mother?

Terry stepped into the awkward pause. "We came here to find a map," he reminded her. "You said you had a plan."

"I'm not sure that it will work."

He took he hand and led her into the Spanish-language collection. "Let's find a treasure map," he said.

Chapter Ten

*A*llison sat at her desk and stared absently at her blank computer screen. She hadn't tapped anything into the monitor for over an hour. The ceiling fan in her small office room hummed quietly, softly rippling the air.

With a sigh, she stood from the desk and switched on a radio atop the bookcase. A top-forty song filled the room, but the dance beat didn't cheer her.

The library search had proved fruitless. Allison grimaced as she remembered the seemingly endless rows of books. Searching just the Spanish-language collection would have required weeks, and even then there were no guarantees that the map was hidden there.

If Esteban Montoya had secreted the map in any of the library's English-language collections, it would certainly never be found. At least not by her and Terry. As he had said, the job was endless.

Besides, Mr. Montoya had hidden the map in the hopes that it would be found. Quite possibly, it had been. Allison wondered whether a new owner would realize the significance of the old, hand-drawn map or if it would simply be thrown away.

The air conditioner clicked on, and the grate over the door in her office issued forth a stream of chilled air. She returned to her desk and eyed the blank computer screen disconsolately. She would never finish this book, she thought. There were too many distractions.

Esteban had told his wife that he had hidden a treasure map in a book at the Phoenix City Library, but he hadn't told her the name of the book. It just didn't ring true. Maybe Mrs. Montoya knew more than she was telling.

Allison ran her fingers lightly over the computer monitor and sighed. The only way to finish the book, she realized, was to continue working. She typed a half-hearted sentence and stopped to read what she had written.

Of course, she realized, there was not even a guarantee that Mr. Montoya had actually even hidden a treasure map in the library.

She forced herself to concentrate on the sentence she had written. She shrugged and wrote another.

She had spent three hours searching the library Monday morning while Terry was at work. She had riffled through hundreds of books, thousands of pages, working methodically through the long rows and finding nothing. She had spent as much time searching on Tuesday and had emerged with the same results.

The quiet hum of the ceiling-fan motor and the gentle threshing of its blades suddenly seemed to fill the room with noise. Allison read and reread what she had written. She scowled to herself. The problem with her writing, she realized, was that she wasn't applying herself properly.

With a soft moan of resignation, she crossed into her living room, plopped onto the sofa, and dialed Terry's work number.

"I'm about ready to give up," she said after saying hello.

Terry's voice held a jocular tone. "Don't do that," he cajoled her. "What's the problem?"

She described her growing sense of hopelessness over the failure of her library searches.

"We've only begun," he said at last. "Think about how long it took searchers to locate the Titanic."

She knew that he was right, and quitting had never been a part of her nature. But she had obligations to a number of magazines to complete articles, and the search for lost gold had put her novel on hold as well.

"I have to think of my finances," she told him. "I have some money saved, and, of course, I'm receiving paychecks in the mail for pieces I've written over the past six months. But if I don't start writing and submitting to magazines soon, the checks are going to stop coming."

The line was silent as she waited for a response from Terry. Hearing nothing, she continued. "It just seems as though we're chasing ghosts. I don't know if I can afford to search for something that may not even exist."

"Now you're beginning to sound like me," Terry said.

She laughed. "I guess that you just started making sense to me."

"I could say the same thing about you," Terry countered. "Maybe there is something behind Mrs. Montoya's story."

"I have to make a decision," Allison said. "Either I'm going to go full-steam ahead on this thing, or I'm going to drop it, or at least put it on a back burner. It's robbing me of my concentration. I haven't written anything for days."

"Don't simply shelve it," Terry advised. "If the search is getting you down, maybe we should think of another avenue to explore."

"That's for sure. I feel as though I've worn my thumb to the bone, flipping through all those books."

"Do you have any ideas?"

Allison rubbed an index finger over the top of the cherrywood end table. "I think that Mrs. Montoya may be holding something back about the location of the map. Did you notice how she seemed to evade our questions when we asked her if she knew where it was?"

"She did seem a little cagey," Terry concurred.

"I want to pay her another visit. Maybe I'll be able to learn a little more this time."

"You think you might be able to pry something out of her?"

"I'm used to conducting interviews," Allison answered. "If I can just earn Mrs. Montoya's confidence, I'm certain that I'll learn something more."

"I don't know." Terry sounded doubtful. "She told us about the gold, she told us about Pablo Ramirez and the Evil One, and she told us about the map. Why would she keep its exact location a secret?"

Allison tried to dismiss Terry's skepticism, but the

same thought had occurred to her. "All I can do is try," she said at last.

"I guess there are only two ways this will work out," Terry replied.

"That's right. Either Mrs. Montoya will tell me where the map is hidden and we launch a search for the gold, or—"

"Mrs. Montoya tells you nothing new," he said, finishing her thought. "Then what do we do?"

She remained silent for a moment. "If Mrs. Montoya doesn't know where the map is hidden," she decided, "we'll have to give up the search for a while."

The crowded streets of Nogales were filled with the vague familiarity Allison felt whenever she returned to a town she had visited long enough to remember but not to remember distinctly. She guided her compact slowly through the crowded streets and crazy traffic.

At least she was able to use her air conditioner on this trip. Terry's open Jeep could feel like an oven on slow-moving streets. Cool air rushed through vents on the dashboard and washed her body.

The narrow alleyway that she and Terry had used as a shortcut appeared on her left, and she turned into it. Her small car required less space than Terry's Jeep, but she still proceeded with great caution as she eased the vehicle down the narrow roadway.

The remainder of the drive passed with relative ease. She drove past the police station and wound through the roads of Nogales until she located the street on which Mrs. Montoya lived.

The red-brick apartment building across from the

Montoyas' home grew larger as she drew nearer. The home of the Ramirez brothers.

Suddenly Allison gasped. Where once the Montoyas' house had stood, there were now only the charred remains of the building's frame.

Allison slowed to a crawl and pulled up at the curb in front of the burned-out structure. The roof had collapsed into the framework, and the concrete foundation was scorched black. Broken glass littered the front yard, joining a mammoth confusion of scorched paper and debris.

A sinking feeling formed in the pit of her stomach. The fire, she was certain, had been no accident. Her eyes roamed the blackened skeleton of the home, then ventured to the apartments across the street. Pablo Ramirez. Was he responsible? Was he the Evil One?

She bit her lip as awful thoughts of Mrs. Montoya's fate raced through her mind. She had seen the work of the Evil One. She had seen how he had pursued a man through the desert until that man had died of thirst.

She walked slowly across the front yard, over the broken glass. Shards snapped brittlely under her feet. The sun pounded down upon the burned-out home, but even in the bright light of day Allison feared the shadows in the home. In the midday heat she felt a chill of dread.

She slowly circled the wreckage of the Montoya home, not knowing what she expected to find, and found nothing.

Suddenly a man's voice shouted angrily at her in accented English from across the street. "What are you doing there?"

Allison whirled at the sound. A short, stocky Mexican man was hurrying across the street from the apartment building, a scowl spread across his face.

"What's your business?" he asked as he stormed across the debris-strewn front yard.

Allison regained her composure. "I'm a friend of the Montoyas," she responded coolly. She turned her back on him and surveyed the burned-out home, stalling for time. Who was this man? "There's been a fire," she said.

"A fire? No kidding. You're a real genius, lady. What gave it away?"

Whoever he was, Allison disliked him immediately.

"You're a friend?" he asked brusquely.

"That's right."

"What's your name?"

"What's yours?" She made a point of staring over his head at the apartment buildings across the street.

"You don't know me?" the man asked, feigning incredulity. "Well, you're going to, lady. I'm Pablo Ramirez, and you're trespassing on my land."

A shudder crawled up Allison's spine. Her mouth was suddenly dry. This was the man Mrs. Montoya suspected of killing both her son and her husband.

"If you don't leave, I'll have you thrown in jail." He sneered at her. "Have you ever spent time in a Mexican prison?"

Allison struggled to maintain her composure. She told herself that she had nothing to fear on this street in the middle of the day. "Do you have any idea where I might find Mrs. Montoya?" she asked.

"Do *you?*" he responded in an accusatory tone. "You tell her when you see her that if she don't buy this land by the end of the month, she's out. We're tired of playing games with her. She has two weeks; then she can find a new place to live." He eyed Allison angrily.

"I don't have any idea where Mrs. Montoya is," she said evenly. "But when I find her, I'll be sure to give her your message."

"Tell her that hiding won't make us go away. She has two weeks. Now get off my land." Pablo Ramirez shot her a look that dared her to remain where she was.

Allison considered standing her ground but realized that she had nothing to gain from a confrontation with Pablo Ramirez. His lips were drawn back into an ugly sneer that exposed uneven teeth. He looked like a murderer, she thought.

She drove slowly down the street, watching Ramirez in her rearview mirror as he crossed back to the red-brick apartment buildings. Her initial shock at finding the Montoya home in ruins had passed. At least she had been able to gather from Ramirez that Mrs. Montoya had not been killed in the blaze, though she couldn't be certain whether she had escaped injury. But where was she hiding?

Allison circled the block. The black roof of the home nearest the Montoyas shimmered in the heat. The neighbors might know Mrs. Montoya's whereabouts, Allison reasoned.

She parked her car two blocks away in an effort to conceal her presence from the prying eyes of Pablo Ramirez, then walked back to the neighbor's house.

Her knock was answered by an elderly woman about Mrs. Montoya's age, slender, pretty, and dressed in a light-blue summer dress.

Allison immediately registered the woman's surprise and introduced herself as a friend of Mrs. Montoya.

At the mention of her neighbor's name, the elderly woman's face took on a grave expression. "I am Yolanda Diaz," she said. Her eyes darted over Allison's shoulder and scanned the street cautiously. "How do you know Rosa Montoya?" she asked, her voice edged with suspicion.

Quickly Allison related what she knew about Esteban Montoya's death. Not knowing whether Mrs. Diaz was familiar with the legend of the Confederate gold and not wanting to give away much information, she simply explained the purpose of her trip as a friendly visitation.

"But I see that her house has been destroyed by a fire," Allison finished. "I hope Mrs. Montoya was not injured."

Mrs. Diaz watched Allison carefully as she spoke. "It was a tragedy," she said quickly when Allison had finished speaking.

Allison stood on the doorstep, waiting for Mrs. Diaz to continue.

"You say you are a friend?" Mrs. Diaz asked at length.

"*Sí.* "

"You will wait here," Mrs. Diaz instructed and closed the door abruptly. Allison heard the scrape of a deadbolt as the elderly woman slipped the lock.

Puzzled, Allison waited on the doorstep. The sun beat upon her back, and perspiration began to glide across her forehead.

Suddenly the lock snapped, and the door opened. Mrs. Diaz faced Allison with a wide smile. "Excuse me,

señorita," she said graciously. "But I had to be certain
that you were who you said you were."

"I'm not sure that I understand. . . ."

"Please come in."

Allison entered the modest home.

"I have just spoken with Señora Montoya on the
phone," Mrs. Diaz explained. "She assures me that you
are a friend."

"Then she wasn't hurt in the fire?" Allison asked
with relief.

"The only damage was to the home," Mrs. Diaz said.
"And you saw for yourself that the damage was complete." She paused. "The fire broke out in the middle
of the night. Fortunately she had been awakened by a
sound and was able to escape injury."

Allison was relieved to learn that Rosa was okay. She
glanced across the vacant lot that separated the Diaz
and Montoya homes. The jumbled collection of burned
posts that had once been the Montoya house jutted in-
congruously from the ground.

"She attempted to notify the fire department, but the
phone was not in operation. Later," Mrs. Diaz continued, "it was discovered that the line had been cut."

"Cut?" Allison exclaimed.

Mrs. Diaz nodded. "The fire burned quickly and
completely. It was an old house, and, I am afraid, these
homes are not constructed to withstand the ravages of
a fire."

"Then it was arson," Allison stated.

"The investigators could find no proof," Mrs. Diaz
said. "It is believed that the fire started with a short in
the fuse box on the outside wall of the house. They

would say only that the phone had been tampered with."

Allison mulled this information over. "No proof," she repeated.

Miss Diaz hesitated. "Do you know of the circumstances surrounding the death of dear old Esteban?"

Allison averted her eyes momentarily. "Yes."

"There was no proof of foul play in that case, either, nor in the case of young Pancho's tragic death."

Allison shook her head mutely.

"You can understand my suspicions when you appeared," Mrs. Diaz said apologetically. "I have never seen you before, and with all these happenings. . . ." Her voice trailed off.

Suddenly the front door opened, and a young woman of about Allison's age entered.

Mrs. Diaz smiled. "My daughter Maria," she said, introducing her to Allison.

Maria nodded mutely and walked quickly from the room.

"Forgive her," Mrs. Diaz said. "She has not been the same since Pancho disappeared. They were engaged to be married." She shook her head. "These things take time." She smiled sadly.

"You needn't apologize," Allison told her. "I understand completely." She wondered how it would feel to lose someone she loved, and Terry's face crossed her mind.

"Rosa asked me to tell you where she was staying," Mrs. Diaz said. "She is in hiding now, and her location must remain a secret. I have told no one her whereabouts, not even my own daughter."

She stopped speaking and waited for Allison to respond.

"Her secret is safe," Allison promised. "I wish only to speak with her."

"Then I will tell you where she may be found," Mrs. Diaz said and outlined the directions to Mrs. Montoya's new home.

As she exited the Diaz home, Allison glanced to the street and felt a quick shock of fear. Parked in the road, directly in front of the house, was a small red car. The same color car that had followed her and Terry to Tucson.

She immediately shifted her gaze to the apartments across the street, searching for a glimpse of Pablo Ramirez, but saw only children playing soccer.

The car appeared to be empty. The windows were rolled tight.

Apparently noticing Allison's hesitation on the doorstep, Mrs. Diaz asked, "Is something wrong?"

Allison smiled quickly. "No," she said. She was letting her imagination get the better of her. On second glance, she noticed several red cars parked along the street. Still, the sudden appearance of the car unnerved her. "Could you tell me," she asked, slightly embarrassed for feeling so paranoid, "whose car that is?"

"The red one?"

Allison nodded.

"It's my daughter's car," Mrs. Diaz replied with a curious tone. "Why do you ask?"

The daughter. Of course. Maria had walked in on them while they were talking. Feeling sheepish, Allison replied, "No reason. I was just curious."

Mrs. Diaz nodded her head vaguely.

Allison made her good-byes and quickly walked the two blocks to her car.

Rosa Montoya's one-room apartment was located on the second floor of an adobe-block apartment building at the end of an alley near the center of Nogales.

Fearing that she might inadvertently reveal Mrs. Montoya's hiding place, Allison had taken special precautions to ensure that she could not be followed. She had parked her car several blocks from the apartment building and had cut through several plazas and crowds in a serpentine route to the home. By the time she had arrived, she was certain that no one, not even the mysterious Evil One, could have shadowed her.

Mrs. Montoya sat slumped in a worn easy chair in the center of the room. The windows of the cramped apartment were open, but no fan circulated the hot air. She smiled wearily at Allison's question.

"*Sí,*" she said. "It was the Ramirez brothers, the twins, Pablo and Simon, who burned my home. They know that I have no insurance. They are trying to force me to sell my land so they may build their new apartment, but I tell you I never will."

"But the police," Allison interjected. "Surely they can help you."

"The police? Chief Perez will help no one who will not pay to be helped." Mrs. Montoya laughed bitterly. "The police are well aware of the Ramirez brothers and their shady business dealings," she said with a derisive smile. "It is the Ramirez brothers who pay for their children's clothes and who buy anniversary gifts for their wives."

Allison told of her encounter with Pablo Ramirez.

"It is good that you left before he called the police. He would have taken pleasure in seeing you arrested."

"He is a vile man," Allison said.

"Yes. I am certain that he is responsible for the deaths of my husband and son. But his brother is worse. They are identical twins, but Simon is the younger. He takes pride in saying that he is two minutes younger but two times tougher than his brother."

Allison shook her head. "I'm glad I didn't run into him."

"You are lucky," Mrs. Montoya agreed. "He would not have warned you before calling the police. It is easy to tell Simon. He has an ugly scar across his nose. The result of a knife fight several years ago."

They were silent for a moment. "What will you do?" Allison asked.

Mrs. Montoya seemed to consider the problem for a few moments, then suddenly her face crumpled. "I have no idea," she cried, burying her face in her hands. "Six months ago I had everything—a husband, a son, and a home. Now I have this." She raised her face and surveyed her Spartan surroundings disconsolately. "Now," she proclaimed in a weak and aged voice, "I have nothing."

Allison crossed the stained white-tile floor and dropped to her knees. She gripped Rosa's hand in hers. "I'm so sorry," she said.

"It is not your fault."

"Is there anything, anything at all that I can do to

help?" Allison asked, mentally calculating how much money she could withdraw from her checking account to aid the grieving woman.

Mrs. Montoya lifted her eyes and met Allison's sympathetic gaze. "You can find the treasure."

Her candid response caught Allison off guard. "I'm afraid we may never be able to do that," she said, for the first time remembering that she had come to Nogales to ask Mrs. Montoya for more information.

"I think you *will* be able to," Mrs. Montoya insisted. "I did not want to draw you into this. I hoped you would lose interest in the legend. But you believe in the gold as my husband believed, and as my son. It has caused much heartache, and I pray you will escape the pain I now suffer.

"You see, I no longer have a choice. I must have the gold. I must pay the Ramirez brothers. And, most important, I must prove that the gold is not a dream. I must know that my family was not murdered in vain."

Allison was momentarily silent. It was imperative now that she find the gold. Further, from her tone, it was clear that Mrs. Montoya knew more about the location of the map than she had previously admitted. "Then you can help us?" Allison asked.

"I pray that you will be able to avoid the fate that befell my family."

"We must have the map," Allison said, imparting a sense of urgency to her words.

Mrs. Montoya smiled wearily. "You must find the treasure. It is my only hope. Even the modest rent I pay for this apartment is too much. I never worried about such things before. My home was paid for, but not the land, and now I have so little money."

Allison nodded. "We can help you," she said sincerely.

Mrs. Montoya met her gaze, and Allison detected new strength in her brown eyes. "I can tell you exactly where the map is hidden. During his lifetime my husband never visited the library. When he finally decided to hide the map in Phoenix, he chose the library so that anyone who happened upon the chosen book might find it. But he found it difficult to simply leave the map in a book and walk away. It was, after all, a piece of family history.

"I have never visited the library in Phoenix, but Esteban told me how large it was. He was afraid that he might hide the map in a book and never again be able to locate it. So he picked his hiding place with care. He noticed that all the books were filed according to a number on their spine."

Allison nodded. "The Dewey decimal system," she said absently.

"Yes. He chose a number that he was certain he would never forget, should he wish to return for the map." She stopped talking and gazed at Allison.

"What was the number?" Allison asked quietly, battling the excitement welling inside her.

Mrs. Montoya smiled. "It is very simple," she said. "123.45."

The sun had set by the time Allison bade farewell to Mrs. Montoya, who had seemed to be almost starved for companionship. Allison had been more than happy to spend time with her and had even gone grocery shopping and had prepared a delicious dinner for them to share.

She had been surprised to learn that Rosa had worked as a dancer in Mexico City and had sung for a time with a big band when the swing sound had swept the big city years earlier.

The dark streets of downtown Nogales were unfamiliar to Allison. Landmarks that had been obvious in the light of day were invisible on the poorly lit streets, and street signs were all but invisible.

She drove slowly through the web of roads. The crowds that had mobbed the streets by day were gone now, replaced by a few tough individuals who skulked in shadows or congregated in small, rough-looking groups.

She cruised slowly through an intersection. A man on the corner yelled something in her direction, then laughed loudly. Her windows were rolled tight, but she checked her doors to ensure that they were locked. Cool air pumped from vents in the dashboard.

She drove on slowly, past a pair of men arguing in front of a dimly lit cantina. She chewed her lip nervously and searched the road, looking for familiar sights.

She was beginning to feel desperate by the time she realized that she had wound her way back to Mrs. Montoya's old neighborhood.

Lights shone in the windows of the Ramirez brothers' apartment building. She cruised slowly past the burned rubble of Mrs. Montoya's home and pulled to a stop in front of Mrs. Diaz's house. Maria's car was still parked in the street, though it had been moved to the other side of the road and was now at the curb before the apartment building.

She breathed a sigh of relief as she approached the front door to ask for directions home. Mariachi music floated gaily through an open window. Mrs. Diaz drew an outline map as her daughter sat silently before a black-and-white TV, watching a musical. The night was less threatening in familiar surroundings, and soon she would be on the freeway home.

Allison had not been driving long before she spotted the brightly lit police headquarters on the street ahead. Floodlights buried in the ground around the structure cast the building in a white glow and lit the grass a bright green.

She drove past. A pickup cruised slowly in the opposite direction. The next left would take her down the alley that would connect her with the main road out of town.

She cranked the steering wheel and turned into the alley. Her headlights washed the walls of the buildings lining the narrow roadway as she pulled in. The night seemed to have narrowed the alleyway, and she was forced to slow to a crawl. The buildings crowded her; their dark walls seemed to press against her, making her feel slightly claustrophobic. She eased her way slowly through the alley.

At last she cleared the exit and nosed into the street that would take her to the border. She glanced into her rearview mirror, and her heart stopped. Another car had turned down the alley. Its headlights shone in her mirror.

Suddenly she was caught in the glare of a set of high-intensity spotlights that blazed through her windshield.

The throaty roar of a hopped-up engine split the night, and the pickup truck that had passed her in front of the police station screeched from its hiding place in the shadows of the street.

Allison stomped on her brakes and jerked forward against her shoulder harness. She turned to shield her eyes from the blinding lights as the truck squealed to a stop inches from her front bumper.

Using her hand as a visor against the glare, she glanced back at the truck in time to see a black-clad figure leap from the truck bed. He crossed the short distance to her car in two easy strides and displayed a large revolver. He wore a black hood as a disguise. "Get out," he ordered in clipped Spanish.

Chapter Eleven

*P*anic welled up inside Allison. She was trapped. The truck blocked her in the front, and the car moving up the alley prevented her from escaping in reverse.

The gunman grabbed her door handle and tugged, but the door was locked. "No!" she screamed. "No! Help me!"

"Open up," she heard him shout through the window. He was speaking Spanish. "Open up, or I'll kill you." He tugged once more on the door handle.

They're going to kill me, she thought. Her only hope was to scare them away. She leaned on her horn. "Help me! Help me!" she screamed. The lights of the car approaching in the alley grew brighter.

Suddenly the gunman turned the butt of the pistol to her window and smashed it.

The tempered window exploded into tiny pebbles of glass that cascaded into the car and peppered the side of Allison's face. "No, no," she screamed. "Get out." Bits of glass fell from her hair.

The gunman's hand ran along the top of the door, fumbling at the lock stem.

118

Allison snatched a pen from her purse and stabbed at the black-gloved hand.

The gunman yelped with pain as the tip penetrated his flesh, but he managed to flip the lock. With a quick motion he had her door open. "You're coming with me," he said, tugging her arm.

Allison lurched halfway out the door but became entangled in the shoulder strap she was wearing. The fabric wound around her neck as the gunman tugged on her arm, trying with brute strength to free her from the restraints.

She could no longer scream. The shoulder harness tightened around her throat, cinching down on her windpipe. *He's going to strangle me,* she thought.

She was aware of the headlights growing brighter behind her, then of the honking of an automobile horn. "What's going on?" she heard someone call.

The gunman gave her arm one last vicious tug. "You were lucky this time," he said and turned and ran back to the pickup truck. The horn continued to sound from the car that had approached in the alley.

The truck's engine revved.

Suddenly gunshots punctuated the scene. Allison slumped against her shoulder harness, half out of her car, drained of strength, and hid behind her open door for cover.

Her windshield flew to pieces and collapsed as several bullets punched holes through the glass. The truck roared off into the distance.

She tugged at the seat belt looped around her neck and felt herself breathing again. Moving slowly, she managed to climb back into her seat. She slumped heavily against the upholstery, gasping for breath.

She was aware that the honking had quieted behind her, and when she looked up, she saw a stranger staring at her through the open car door, his expression a mixture of fear and puzzlement.

"Caramba," he said. "What happened to you?"

Allison and Terry were seated in the office of Chief Perez of the Nogales police department. He glanced at each of them with deep-brown eyes that belied no hint of his thoughts, then turned to his deputy, Officer Alvarez, who stood beside the chief's desk.

He returned his gaze to Terry. "It is good that you could arrive so quickly," he said. "We have no facilities to transport Miss Ames beyond the border. I am certain that she would like to return home."

Terry's face was stern. His eyes never wavered from the captain. "You don't seem to have the facilities for much of anything," he pointed out.

Perez assumed a pained expression and gestured with his hands. "I have explained over and over again, these are dangerous times in Nogales. Drug bandits roam the streets at will. We are a poor city, without the resources of your American cities, and we are unable to maintain a police force capable of stopping *all* crime within our borders."

Allison rubbed a hand over her face. *I must be a mess,* she thought. She had been crying and was exhausted from the excitement and lack of sleep. Her neck was badly bruised, and her arm felt as if it had been wrenched from its socket.

After a cursory examination by a doctor, in which she had been pronounced bruised but fit, she had waited alone in the police station for Terry to make the drive from Phoenix to Nogales. He had finally arrived at four o'clock in the morning.

Just as they had been leaving, they had been summoned to the chief's office for questioning. "I personally handle all cases involving Americans," he had said. What had followed had been a lengthy interrogation.

Terry leaned forward in his seat. "She was attacked, almost kidnapped, faced a gun, and had her car destroyed, and you tell me that there's nothing you can do until daybreak?"

"You needn't shout, señor," Officer Alvarez replied firmly. "These drug soldiers are dangerous *bandidos.*"

Allison watched him as he spoke. He was tall, skinny, and sinister looking. She had taken an immediate dislike to him.

"It would be perilous," he continued, "to send my men out in a search before the light of day."

Terry raised his voice still further. "Who said anything about drug soldiers? We've told you about the gold, the Evil One, and Pablo Ramirez. That's where your answers lie."

An angry look crossed the chief's face. "Your accusations are meaningless," he said. "And you would be advised to think twice before blackening the name of one of the proudest families in Nogales."

"The Ramirez name is highly respected here," Officer Alvarez added. "You had better remember that in the future."

"Then you don't plan to do anything?"

"What are we to do?" the deputy asked sternly. "You report murders that you say occurred on American soil. We can do nothing about that. If you have suspicions, you should report them to your authorities in Arizona."

"I'm talking about the attempted kidnapping of my friend," Terry said. His eyes met the deputy's and didn't flinch.

"Kidnapping, again kidnapping," Chief Perez uttered wearily. "All for some rumored lost treasure." He shook his head and eyed Allison. "Once again, Miss Ames, what is your business in Nogales?"

Allison inhaled deeply. Would this never end? "I've answered that question several times. I was visiting Rosa Montoya."

Alvarez crossed the floor and took up a position behind Allison and Terry. They were forced to watch him over their shoulders. "But you do not tell us where she lives. Why, Miss Ames? I want to know, why?"

Allison cleared her throat. "As I've explained over and over, she wishes that to remain secret." She licked her lips. She had decided upon first entering the police station that she would not reveal Mrs. Montoya's location. The Ramirez brothers were obviously friendly with the local constabulary, and Allison had no desire to endanger her by revealing her whereabouts. The image of the burned-out house was still clear in her mind.

"It looks rather . . . suspicious," Chief Perez said. "Only drug bandits roam the streets so late at night."

A knock sounded at the door, and a smartly uniformed clerk entered. He crossed to the chief's desk and whispered in his ear. The chief nodded, and the clerk spun and departed.

"Well," Perez finally said, "after a thorough search, your car has revealed no trace of contraband. Therefore—"

"Contraband?" Terry exploded. "You've been going over her car looking for drugs? Haven't you listened to a single word we've said?"

Perez smiled thinly. "Relax, señor. No one is above suspicion, especially those who are driving through alleyways in the dark of night."

Terry looked as though he were ready to continue the argument, but Allison glanced in his direction and shook her head. It was obvious that they could expect no help from the Nogales police department.

Terry inhaled deeply to swallow his anger and stared stonily at the chief.

"If you have no other business in Nogales," the chief said, shifting his attention to Allison, "you are free to go."

"Thank you," she said, standing.

"In the future," he continued, "you would be wise to travel during daylight hours."

Terry placed his hand on Allison's waist and steered her toward the door.

The deputy watched them through slitted eyes, barely concealing his suspicion as they exited.

The lights of the border crossing grew brighter, and Allison was able to distinguish the blue-uniformed customs officers as Terry's Jeep drew nearer to the banks of gates that separated the Mexican side of Nogales from the American side.

They had decided to pay a nominal fee and allow the Nogales police to keep Allison's car in their impound lot until they were able to return and make the necessary repairs. In its present state, with its windshield blown out, it would never have been permitted across the border.

"I don't know how they could have followed me," Allison said. "I went to extremes to make certain that no one was on my tail when I visited Mrs. Montoya."

Terry shook his head. "That's the puzzle. There's always the possibility that the Evil One wasn't involved at all. Maybe it *was* drug soldiers. You said there were two working together. As far as we know, the Evil One works alone." His voice held the barest hint of doubt, as though even he weren't convinced by his words.

"Not if the Evil One is Pablo Ramirez," Allison pointed out. "He has a brother named Simon." She informed Terry of what she had learned about the Ramirez family. "They've teamed up on this. I'm sure of it. I just wish I knew how they managed to follow me."

The conversation lapsed into silence for several moments while they considered possibilities.

"That's it," Allison exclaimed, snapping her fingers.

"What's it?"

"I got lost driving from Mrs. Montoya's apartment and ended up asking Mrs. Diaz for directions back to the border. She lives across from the apartment building where the Ramirez brothers live. They could have seen me pull up."

"You're right," Terry said, his voice grim. "The Ramirez brothers must have been behind the attack."

"And the murders," Allison intoned quietly.

"If the Ramirezes are involved, we can't count on the police helping us," Terry said. "You saw how they feel about the Ramirez family."

"And the police in Arizona won't help us with a murder investigation. They don't even believe that a murder has been committed."

They again fell into silence. Terry drummed his fingers against the steering wheel. "I've got a gun stashed on the other side," he said at last, indicating the far side of the border with a jerk of his head. "Can't cross the border with one, but when I got your phone call, I decided it would be our best insurance on the road between here and Phoenix."

Allison nodded silently. After the events of the evening, she couldn't have agreed more.

The Jeep slowed as Terry pulled into a border-entry port. A customs agent surveyed the Jeep from behind a glass window in his cubicle, punched some information into a desktop computer, watched the screen momentarily, then exited onto the cement driveway. "Good morning," he said, glancing from Terry to Allison. His eyes lingered on her bruises for several seconds.

Oh, please, Allison thought, *not another delay.* She was tired and wanted only to get back to her comfortable bed in Mesa.

She was relieved when the customs agent asked just the standard questions regarding the transportation of fruits and merchandise on which duty was owed, and flagged them through the border.

Terry drove silently for a mile before pulling in at a dingy-looking motel.

As exhausted as she was, Allison found herself on the defensive. "What's this all about?" she asked him.

"I've got a room."

"One room?"

"That's all that's necessary," he said with a laugh.

"You'd better think again."

"It's not for us," Terry said, jumping from the Jeep.

He and Allison crossed the narrow parking lot to Room 17. Terry inserted the key, and they entered a room that was as run-down as the building's shabby exterior.

"I got the room for this," he explained, pushing back the mattress on the bed. His rifle lay atop the box spring. He snatched it up. "Let's go."

Allison looked at him holding the rifle and was suddenly overcome with emotion. She leaned into him, burying her cheek in his chest. She circled her arms under his and gripped his shoulders. She couldn't stop the tears that streamed from her eyes. "I was so scared. I thought they would kill me."

Terry leaned the rifle against a chair and embraced her, stroking her hair with one hand. "It's all right," he whispered in her ear. "It's all over."

She raised her tearstained face to meet his sympathetic gaze. He would protect her, she knew. She smiled weakly. "I'm sorry. I'm just so tired."

"I know."

Impulsively she stood on her toes and kissed him softly on the lips. "Thank you for being here when I needed you."

He smiled and said, "It's all right."

They stood there for a moment, quietly, holding each other, only the whisper of traffic on the freeway gently tufting the silence. Then she said, "We have to go."

"Right." Terry grabbed the rifle, and they returned to the Jeep.

Despite her ordeal of the night before, despite her lack of sleep, and despite the pain in her swollen throat and aching shoulder, Allison could barely suppress a smile as she and Terry entered the library the next morning. This was to be the final test. Would the information given by Mrs. Montoya prove to be the key that would unlock the mystery of the lost Confederate gold?

She felt certain that the map would be found, but a slight shadow of doubt gave rise to the barest hint of nervous anticipation.

They were the first patrons through the doors, and she felt the librarians and pages eyeing them as they crossed the vacant entry foyer. A studious-looking man with gray hair and steel-rimmed glasses smiled good morning in their direction as she and Terry passed the information desk.

They know, she thought, despite her better judgment. *They know that we have come here to find a treasure map.*

"I feel as if we're being watched everywhere we go," she whispered to Terry as the elevator doors slid closed. "I have to get a hold of myself."

He smiled at her. "If you can't manage, I'll be glad to give it a try." He appeared completely calm, suppressing any excitement he might have been feeling beneath a cool, composed exterior.

"You'll be the first to know if I need a hand," she promised, returning his smile.

The elevator slowed to a stop. "Well," Terry said, gently guiding Allison through the door, his hand on the small of her back, "this is it."

She inhaled deeply, closed her eyes, and raised crossed fingers in reply.

"Let's find out if it's for real," he declared.

They walked toward a shelf of books near the far wall. Allison attempted an air of calm self-assurance, but nagging doubts lingered. What if there was no map? It would mean the end of the search. She would never discover a cache of lost gold. Her life would return to normal. Suddenly the day-to-day routine she had followed before learning the legend of the lost gold seemed somehow mundane. Her fingers were locked crossed.

A small placard near the top of a row of shelving identified a section of books that used the 100 series call number.

Terry inhaled deeply and exhaled slowly through pursed lips. "The moment of truth," he said.

Allison's stomach lurched with anticipation. Even Terry's come-what-may facade was evaporating. They walked along the rows of books, eyes glued to the spines, reading the call numbers. It was all she could do to keep herself from running down the aisle.

"110.23," Terry said absently as they passed through the aisle. "116.7. We're getting closer."

No longer able to contain her excitement, she

grabbed Terry's wrist. "Hurry up!" She tugged him down the row.

He continued to read aloud the numbers on the spines. "120.5 . . . 121.38 . . . 122.7."

Allison traced her fingers along the spines of the books. 123.45 would be here; she was sure of it. A call number beginning with 123 caught her attention. Her index finger jumped across the spines of the books on the shelf. 123.3, 123.34, 123.4, 123.77. Her heart seemed to stop beating. She reread the numbers on the spines of the books she had just passed, but 123.45 was nowhere to be found.

She turned to Terry. His face mirrored her own disappointment. "It isn't here," she said.

"It must be." He stepped forward and scanned the shelf.

She reread the numbers on the spines of the books. It had to be here. They had gone through so much.

Suddenly an awful thought crossed her mind. "What if the book has been checked out? The map will be lost."

Terry stood staring at the bookshelves.

She licked her lips as her eyes darted back and forth along the shelves, scanning Dewey decimal numbers.

"Look at this," Terry said suddenly, stooping down and sliding a cardboard-bound volume from a shelf near the floor.

Allison leaned forward. Something in the tone of his voice gave her hope. "What is it?" she asked, unable to allow herself the benefit of believing that he had located the missing book.

Terry stood up and turned to her. He held the book in his hand. "123.45 CR," he said. He read the title and handed her the thin volume. "I don't think we ever had to worry about this one being on loan."

Her heart began to pound. It had been misshelved. She felt as though her emotions were riding a roller coaster—one minute up, the next down, and now, again, up. Her hand began to tremble. She read the cover: *Determinism and Indeterminism: Chance, Free Will, and Freedom.*

With a deep breath Allison folded back the cover. She nearly yelped with excitement. A piece of tattered parchment, creased and folded, slipped from the book to the floor.

Terry snatched it up and carefully opened the aged paper. Allison crowded his side as he worked. When he was finally done, they knew that they had found what they had been searching for. They were eyeing a crude map.

Chapter Twelve

*T*wo weeks passed. Allison's injuries had almost completely healed. Only a green-tinged bruise remained around her throat where the seat belt had nearly strangled her, and her shoulder was only slightly stiff in the mornings. Her car, too, had been repaired. A new windshield had been installed at a garage in Nogales, and Terry had followed her home in his Jeep.

She and Terry had visited several prospecting-supply stores and outfitted themselves for their trek into the desert with lightweight packs, freeze-dried foods, several canteens, and a collapsible dolly that might be useful if a large cache of gold were discovered.

The Mojave's bleak scenery hadn't changed since they had first discovered the dying Esteban Montoya. Standing scant feet from where his body had been found, Allison watched as Terry scrambled down the side of the now-familiar sand dune. The desert, she thought, probably hadn't changed much at all in the over one hundred years since Pedro Montoya had hidden his treasure here.

"I can't figure it out," Terry said, breathing heavily

and wiping his brow. "The landmarks on this map don't make any sense." He stared at the sky, a thoughtful expression on his face, and handed his map to Allison.

They had made several copies of it, in case something happened to the original, and she studied the rumpled, sweat-stained sheet in her hand.

"Of course," he added, "it was just a hunch, coming out here again. But it only makes sense to suppose that Esteban Montoya died somewhere in the vicinity of the gold."

"Maybe he was having trouble reading the map too," she suggested.

"You mean, you think that maybe he wasn't exactly sure where the gold was?"

Allison shrugged. The possibility had occurred to both of them while planning the expedition. Perhaps Esteban Montoya had been combing the desert, attempting to locate landmarks identified on the map. He may never have been close to actually discovering the treasure.

"I'm sure that he knew where the gold was," Terry said with certainty. "All the landforms noted on this map are located in this area."

Allison's eyes widened with interest.

"Look here," he continued, laying his index finger across the map in her hands. "This series of ridges lies to the northeast of our position, but it's drawn to the northwest on the map."

"How can we be sure that these are the same ridges?"

"We can't be. Not one hundred percent. But we have a sand dune here." He indicated with his finger. "Which must be the sand dune I just climbed. There aren't many around here." He was silent for a moment. "Those ridges to the northeast are located to the northwest on the map, and this peak, due east, is shown on the map as being directly west of our position."

Allison chewed her lip. Though she knew she might risk angering Terry if she voiced her doubts, she thought it might prove useful to explore all sides of the situation before wasting valuable time searching an area that didn't closely match the map.

"A lot of this desert looks the same," she said. "Isn't it possible that we've simply stumbled upon an area that resembles the section outlined in the map?"

"Not likely." Terry turned in a slow circle, studying the terrain of the wash. "It's here. We're on top of it. And so was Esteban Montoya. He was this close." He gestured, pressing his thumb and forefinger together. "But then he realized that he was being followed. He wandered in this area for who knows how long, circling the gold, but never once giving the location of the treasure away."

A chilling thought suddenly struck Allison. "How do we know that he didn't give the location away? Maybe he did. Maybe he was killed *after* finding the gold."

Terry shook his head. "Didn't happen that way," he said simply.

Terry's confidence did little to assuage Allison's doubts, however. "It makes sense," she insisted. "The killer stalked him until Mr. Montoya found the gold. After that. . . ." Her voice trailed off. "Well, we know what happened after that." She paused a moment. "The gold has probably been raided."

"Hasn't been," Terry said.

Allison, finding herself becoming irritated by Terry's matter-of-fact frankness, asked, "And just how can you be so sure?"

"In the first place, someone, probably the same person responsible for the deaths of Mr. Montoya and his son, has been trying to steal this map from us ever since we first visited Nogales."

Allison felt slightly sheepish. Of course. And the attempted kidnapping in Mexico had been another attempt to locate the gold. She rubbed her neck where the belt had choked her. She wouldn't allow her imagination to run away like that again.

"Okay," she said. "You're right. Do you have anything else?"

Terry scratched his head. "You forget, I'm a geologist. I'm used to roaming the desert. I've developed a sort of sixth sense about traveling out here. I notice things."

"What have you noticed so far?"

"Well, I've noticed that we're being followed."

Despite the heat Allison felt her blood flow cold. "Followed?" she asked, her voice a whisper, as though the mysterious interloper might hear what she was saying.

"He's not that close," Terry said with a wry smile. He nodded at the dune. "I spotted him from the top just a few minutes ago. He was glassing us from the crest of a wash a mile or so away."

"What do you mean, 'glassing us'?"

Terry looked at her, then glanced back in the direction of their tail. "He was using a spotting scope, a small telescope, to watch our moves."

"If he was so far away, how did you see him? He would have been barely more than a speck at that distance."

"You're right. But the sun reflected off the lens of his scope. It was unmistakable. Even a small sliver of a mirror can be used by travelers lost in the desert to signal for help. That lens was probably the size of the bottom of a soda bottle. It looked like a star out there." He scratched absently at his neck. "It was unmistakable," he repeated.

Allison let the information sink in. They were being followed by a killer, a man who had struck twice at his victims in the borderless frontiers of the Mojave Desert and had left two corpses lying in the dust.

"One thing's for sure," Terry was saying. "If Mr. Montoya *had* led him to the gold, we wouldn't have a tail right now."

Allison took a deep breath to calm her nerves. They had always anticipated that they would be followed into the desert, but suddenly Terry's sighting of the killer had driven the danger home. They were targets now.

She found herself wishing that they had never become embroiled in the search for the treasure. Mrs. Montoya had warned them.

Terry's pack lay where he had dropped it under a mesquite tree. He stopped to shoulder it. "I'm glad we spotted him," he said. "At least we know now where he is. And we've got something neither Mr. Montoya nor his son had when they were doing their searching."

He tapped the butt of his rifle against the revolver holstered at his side. "We've got insurance."

Allison remained silent.

Terry noticed her apprehension. "We can turn back right now. The gold has been here for over one hundred years; it will still be here in a month, a year, even a decade."

"No," Allison said. Despite the obvious danger, or perhaps because of it, her sense of adventure was piqued. "We know where the killer is. His element of surprise is gone."

The search for the gold—and the killer on their tail—would make a great story, she realized. "We've come this far; I say we go all the way."

Terry smiled. His ease helped to take the edge off Allison's nerves. Nothing, it seemed, could frighten him. This was just a camping trip as far as he was concerned. "Let's find some gold," he said.

"First we have to decipher the map," Allison reminded him.

He shook his head. "It's all here." He gestured to the landforms on the map. "But in the wrong position."

Allison mulled the problem silently for a moment. A hot breeze skidded over the desert and tousled her hair. "You said that a series of ridges that lies to the northeast was sketched in to the northwest?"

"That's right."

"And a peak to the east was depicted as being west?"

"Right again. It's as though everything is backward."

She snapped her fingers. "Exactly," she exclaimed. "The map was drawn as a mirror image of the landscape it depicted."

"A mirror image?"

Allison slung her pack off her shoulders, rummaged quickly through a zippered pocket on its front, and extracted her notebook and a pencil. "Esteban Montoya drew the map backward. Everything to the west of the treasure, he placed in the east, and everything to the east, he placed in the west."

"That makes sense. It would confuse anyone who might steal the map."

"Right," Allison said quickly. She was tracing over the lines on the copy of the map, outlining them heavily in pencil.

"What are you doing?" Terry asked.

"Just a minute," Allison responded, working speedily. When she was finished, she dropped her pencil and removed a clean sheet of paper from the notebook. "I'm going to make a mirror image of *this* map."

She placed the map copy she had just outlined face down over the blank sheet of notebook paper and rubbed its back heavily with the heel of her palm.

"You're going to transfer the darkened lines from the map onto the clean sheet of paper." Terry's voice held a tone of admiration.

"And when we're done, we'll have a copy of the map that represents the terrain around this sand dune."

She finished rubbing the paper and lifted it away. The once-clean sheet of notebook paper now held hazy pencil marks that had been transferred from the original map copy.

"Just a few more seconds to make everything clear." Allison sketched over the faint marks with her pencil. "That should do it."

Terry examined the finished product. "You really impress me, Ames," he said, his gaze roaming to the top of the dune. "This looks like it, but there's only one way to be sure." He dropped his pack to the ground. "I'll have to climb it again to check this out."

"I'll race you," Allison teased.

"Not today. I'm afraid you might win."

When they gained the top of the dune, Terry oriented the map to the scenery. He let out a low whistle. "It fits perfectly," he said.

Allison leaned against his shoulder and checked the map to the terrain. She had no trouble locating the series of ridges to the northeast or the peak to the east. In the west a series of dry wash beds appeared exactly as depicted on the map.

Her eyes roamed over the map and locked on the X penciled in to the southwest.

"It's back there," Terry said. "We're being watched. Do as I do," he instructed.

He turned slowly in a circle. Allison followed his lead.

When they were facing to the southwest, he said, "It's out there, somewhere in those cliffs around that mesa."

Allison stared intently at the gray cliffs that seemed to erupt from the desert floor barely a mile from their position.

Terry continued to turn. "Just keep making a circle," he told her. "Our visitor won't know what we're looking for."

Allison continued to turn. "Where is he?" she asked, the hollow feeling of fear spreading through her.

They were facing east. "About a mile away, in that series of razorbacks," Terry said, nodding imperceptibly at a collection of jagged ridges.

Allison eyed the area carefully but could spot no sign of his presence.

They continued to turn slowly. The razorbacks that provided shelter for the killer on their trail disappeared from view. But the sick fear that engulfed Allison left her cold in the desert heat. Would she and Terry ever again emerge from this desert?

Chapter Thirteen

*T*he narrow crevasse offered relief from the blistering desert sun, but the ground was sandy and the rising incline exhausting. Allison followed Terry up the steep, winding wash toward the cliffs that hid the Confederate treasure.

The day had seemed to continue without end. Under Terry's advice they had hiked a twisting, circuitous route toward the cliffs. He had suggested that doing so would not only serve to create the impression that they were not exactly sure what they were looking for, but might help them lose whoever it was that was tailing them.

Allison was breathing hard. They were surrounded by the narrow gorge. Its hard, gray walls sprang vertically on both sides. Aside from a short length of the jagged trail that angled steeply through the rift, all that could be seen was a sliver of blue sky high above.

"We're almost there," Terry said, stopping for a break. Sweat shone on his face.

Despite the heat and the danger, Allison felt her pulse quicken. The Confederate gold. It had once seemed so distant, so remote. It was unbelievable that they should be on the verge of discovering it.

Terry shrugged his pack to the ground and settled in a plot of cool sand under an outcropping of rock. Allison followed his lead. Her back was wet where the pack had been resting, and as she leaned against the shady rock, she felt a gentle cool flow through her body.

"This is where it's going to start getting dangerous," Terry said. "We'll have to play this out carefully if we hope to get the gold."

Allison nodded. "He'll follow us until he's sure that we've found the gold, and then—" She stopped abruptly. She couldn't believe what she was saying. Only now, as they sat on the edge of discovering the gold, did the stark reality of the danger they were in sink in.

Let's go home, she wanted to say, but she remained silent. Too much was riding on their discovery of the gold. She thought of Mrs. Montoya being forced to live alone in that squalid apartment. And she thought of Mr. Montoya and his son, both dead. Both killed. The murderer, at this very moment, was stalking her and Terry.

The killer had to be brought to justice, but the risk was great. The danger descended on her like a shroud.

"I'm scared," she admitted.

Terry glanced at her crossways. "It's risky," he said in his usual offhand manner. "But we can do it."

"Mr. Montoya and his son probably thought they could too."

"We can quit this search any time," he offered without hesitation. His voice held only concern for Allison's fears.

"No," she insisted, her thoughts turning to Mrs. Montoya. She was determined that the old woman should have a new home built and that she should never again face the threat of eviction from her land. It was small recompense for the heartache she had endured, Allison realized, but it was something, at least.

"I know that we'll find the gold," she said.

"We have an advantage over the guy on our tail. We know that he's out there. He's hidden, but he gave himself away when he glassed us. He's lost the element of surprise, and he doesn't know it. That puts an ace up our sleeve."

"How will we take the gold once we uncover it?" Allison asked, no longer entertaining any doubt as to its existence.

Terry winked at her. "That's where we outfox the fox." He pushed at some sand with his boot heel. "Since the killer doesn't know that we're on to him, he'll be expecting us to lead him directly to the gold, but we're going to play it differently. When we find the gold, we're not going to stop to pick it up. We're going to keep on walking as if it weren't even there."

"And then come back for it later," she said, picking up on Terry's strand of thought. "After we've hiked all over the desert to put him off the scent."

He chuckled. "Like we've been doing all day," he concluded, sensing Allison's distaste for the idea. "The object is to confuse our tail. We don't have to exhaust ourselves, though. We'll simply hike until dark, then return under cover of the night to retrieve the gold. If we get lucky and find the gold this afternoon, we'll be back tonight to get it. If we find it tomorrow, we'll be back tomorrow night, and if it's the day after tomorrow, well, you get the picture."

Allison nodded. "We'll set up a camp and act as if we're settling in for the night. The killer will simply think that we have yet to locate the gold and will expect us to sleep through until sunrise. He'll be sleeping when we double back for the gold."

"That's the plan," Terry said with a smile. "Our first problem, though, is locating the gold." He produced the map copy and held it carelessly in his hand. "These old maps weren't drawn up by surveyors. They were sketched out by people who wanted to keep the location of their treasure a secret."

He waved the map at Allison. "This is a perfect example. Not only did Pedro Montoya draw this map as a mirror image of the terrain, he also neglected to exactly locate the treasure. All we know for sure is that it's located somewhere in the cliffs that surround that mesa."

"He probably memorized any landmarks he thought he would need to relocate the treasure," Allison guessed.

"Finding the gold with this map will be difficult but not impossible. The map marks the position at the northernmost edge of the cliffs. That's the section we'll search first."

"It seems that a cave should be pretty easy to find," Allison said, recalling that Pedro Montoya had not buried the gold but secreted it inside a cave.

"Not necessarily. I've crawled through some cave entrances no wider than my shoulders. Caves are rarely the gaping holes in the sides of mountains that Hollywood likes to show us. Usually their entrances are splits or fissures in the earth's surface. And if they are disguised by rocks or boulders, they can be nearly impossible to detect."

"So you expect a long search for the cave entrance?" Allison already dreaded the hours of endless hiking with the heavy pack on her back.

Terry tilted his head. "I won't say it's going to be easy, but I'm not going to say it'll be hard. We'll head up to the northern edge of the caves and begin our search there."

He glanced at Allison. "Are you still scared?"

"No," she answered. Then, after a pause, "Yes."

"We'll be all right." His use of the word "we" comforted her, and she knew that she would be able to face her fears.

Terry stood, dusted the sand from the seat of his pants, and hefted his pack on his back. He shrugged his shoulders, a scowl on his face. "You know," he said, dropping the pack back to the ground, "It might be a good idea to leave a few canteens of water in this gorge. They weigh a lot, and I'm getting tired of hauling them around. We'll be coming back this way on the way home, so we could pick them up then."

He rummaged through his pack and withdrew two blanket-covered canteens. Allison handed him two from her pack.

"We'll hide them in this crack," Terry said, jamming the canteens sideways into a deep fissure in the side of the gorge. "No one will see them, and the rock will keep the water cool."

Allison feigned exhaustion as she pulled her pack over her shoulders. "It's still too heavy," she groaned.

"You look good in a pack," Terry joked.

Allison smiled. "Flattery will get you everywhere," she said.

"I'll remember that." He eyed her silently for a minute before turning and heading up the narrow draw.

Allison followed closely. The look on his face had been new and different. It had been more alluring than ever. She trailed him without speaking, wondering if the same thoughts racing through her mind were racing through his.

The cliffs jutted from the earth and ended abruptly at a flat-topped mesa. Faults and fissure lines in the gray stone gave the impression of a series of dominoes toppled one upon the other. A multitude of trails crisscrossed their way to the top. The craggy walls of the enormous landform provided numerous handholds and ledges for hiking, but splinters of rock and gravel that littered the ground made the going arduous.

Allison leaned her face into the wall and moved sideways along a narrow trail, closely following Terry. They had dropped their packs at a point near the base of the cliff, and she was thankful that she was not balancing that burden in such dangerous terrain. One misstep, she realized, could easily be her last.

She was aware of Terry's breathing ahead of her. It was deep and heavy, imitating her own, she knew. The heat of the afternoon sun radiated from the cliff face, and she dripped perspiration. The strap of the canteen around her neck burned and stung.

"Whoa!" Terry shouted, stumbling over some gravel. The bits of stone skittered across the trail and tumbled over the edge. "Watch your step," he said, looking not at Allison but at the trail immediately before his feet.

Though the trail they were on was at least two feet wide, the outer edge was ragged and weathered and dropped vertically nearly one hundred feet to another narrow, rock-strewn ledge below. Farther down, a dry wash bed lapped at the base of the cliff. Neither Terry nor Allison was willing to risk a fall, so they hugged the simmering cliff face.

Allison picked her way over the spot that had nearly tripped Terry. The shards of rock that littered the trail were like slippery pieces of ice. She placed her feet carefully with each step.

For nearly two hours they picked their way along the faces of the cliffs, searching for the cave. At last the setting sun seemed to indicate that the search would be over for the day.

"He's certain to suspect that we've discovered something here," Allison said as long shadows began to descend on the desert. "We've been hunting through this area for too long."

"You may be right." Terry paused to take a short breath before inching slowly along a particularly narrow section of ridge. He pressed himself nearly flat against the face of the cliff and shuffled over broken rock on the trail to a wider outcropping some six feet away.

"It's been slower than I anticipated," he continued,

turning to face Allison from the relatively wide trail section. "We'll move on up to the end of this trail," he said, jerking his head toward an area approximately one hundred feet away where the trail narrowed significantly before climbing steeply a few feet to the summit of the mesa. "Then we'll return to our packs and set camp."

Allison paused at the narrow trail section Terry had just traversed. "You're not worried that the killer might close in on us if he suspects we're near the treasure?" she asked.

"He wouldn't make the same mistake again," Terry answered, wiping his brow and surveying the surrounding desert from their excellent vantage point. "He has already murdered twice and been left without the treasure. He'll wait until he's sure this time. He must suspect that we may be his last chance to link up with the gold."

Allison only half listened to him. She was eyeing the narrow strip of trail that she had to cross. Compared to this, the rest of the afternoon's hike had been a stroll down Main Street. She wiped her sweating palms against her thighs. "Here goes nothing," she said and skidded her foot forward.

"It's not as tough as it looks," Terry assured her. "Just take it easy. Imagine you're leaning against a wall of your home. Really, it's no different. You have plenty of room."

Allison didn't respond. She was too busy concentrating on keeping her balance. Terry was right, though, she knew, and his presence helped to ease her fears. If she were attempting to cross this trail on flat land, with no danger of injury from a fall, she would give no thought at all to the feat. It was nothing at all.

But she wasn't on flat land, and a misstep could cost her her life. Slowly she inched across the narrow strip of trail, barely breathing for fear that a deep breath would throw her off balance and send her hurtling into the void below.

Her foot skidded over a small patch of gravel. Her heart stopped. Her fingers clawed at the bare rock of the cliff face. *It's all right,* she thought. *There's nothing to this.*

She caught her breath, continued forward, and relaxed somewhat. There really *was* nothing to it. She had performed stunts and acrobatics on balancing beams during her days as a ballerina, and this ledge was much wider than the beam. She continued cautiously but confidently to the other side.

Terry extended his hand and helped her onto the wider ledge. "Safe and sound," he said. He gazed at her for a moment. "Whoops. You're covered with dirt." He began to gently brush at her shoulders, then the backs of her shoulders, then her back.

"I think I can take care of the rest," she said, nudging his hands away. "Later."

"If you need any help, just let me know."

"Have you forgotten why we're here?" she asked. "We're supposed to be searching for a gold mine."

"But look at the view," he said, gesturing in a wide semicircle with his arm.

The splendor of the desert at sunset filled Allison with awe. A blazing orange sun dipped behind purple mountains that blended slowly into pink flatlands, and a warm breeze carried on it the sweet scent of mesquite.

She took a moment to enjoy the view afforded from

her position near the top of the cliffs; then a discomforting thought occurred to her.

"I wonder where he is right now," she said, referring to the killer she knew was lurking somewhere in the lengthening shadows of the coming desert night.

Terry snorted. "You sure know how to break a mood, Ames."

She looked at him, and he was smiling. "Don't you take anything seriously?" she asked.

"Only serious things," he said in his typically blithe manner.

Allison shook her head. Though she pretended to be slightly irritated by Terry's devil-may-care attitude, secretly she was glad that he was able to make light of potentially dangerous situations. His calm helped to put her own edgy nerves at ease.

"We've only got a little more of this ledge left to check over," Terry was saying. "Let's get it done and head back down to make camp. I don't want to be up here when it gets dark."

The tone of his voice gave Allison little hope that the cave would be discovered that day.

Terry moved forward easily a few feet before the ledge narrowed once again and he was forced to hug the cliff face. Though she could have waited for him on the wide section, Allison felt that she should participate as fully as Terry, so she followed closely behind.

She watched as he inched forward, his fingers splayed open along the craggy rock of the cliff. The trail widened again, and he moved forward quickly. Suddenly she saw his lead hand disappear into a shadow.

"We've got something here," he said. He continued

to move slowly forward. "It's a promontory of rock." He spoke in low tones. His entire arm had by now vanished. He moved forward farther still. "It juts out at an angle from the rest of the cliff, so it's impossible to see unless you're right on top of it." He shuffled forward one last foot and stared into the deepening shadow of the promontory. "It's a cave," he said.

Chapter Fourteen

A crescent moon shone clearly in the starry sky, its weak light casting the desert in a faint gray glow. Terry and Allison stood poised at the narrow entrance to the secret cave.

"It looks pretty tight," Terry said. He unlimbered his rifle and handed it to Allison, then turned sideways and wedged himself into the opening. "I'll go first." He wriggled against the rock, forcing himself through the slot. "We'll wait until we're well inside before we turn on our lights. I'll let you know when I'm oriented; then we'll both take a look."

Allison nodded mutely. Her excitement was so great that she didn't trust herself to speak quietly.

Terry slithered into the mouth of the cave. Allison stood silently to the side, holding the rifle awkwardly, breathing quietly and recalling the events of the day.

After having descended from the cliffs earlier that evening, they had set camp. They had cooked a dinner of hot dogs and beans over a campfire and had whiled away the early-evening darkness in quiet conversation around the dying embers of the fire. Anyone watching would not have suspected that they had stumbled upon a great treasure that day.

Terry had suggested, and Allison had agreed, that they should wait until very late, at least until after midnight, before venturing back up the side of the cliff. Their prolonged exploration of the area had undoubtedly aroused the curiosity of the killer who was trailing them, and they wanted to be certain that he was asleep by the time they left.

Terry disappeared into the black shadow that marked the cave opening. Standing on the ledge, Allison could hear pebbles falling inside the cave as Terry squirmed through the first few narrow feet. Then only the night sounds of the desert met her ears.

She waited silently at the mouth of the cave. A cricket chirped mightily from somewhere just up the trail.

After a minute or two she heard Terry rustling once again toward the cave's mouth. The dark silhouette of his head appeared, followed by his shoulders. "It's tight at first," he whispered, "but then it widens out."

He peered down at the holster on his waist. "I'll take the rifle now," he said, reaching for the weapon. "I thought it might be too cramped in here for it. The real problem is with this holster. It keeps jamming against the walls." He smiled at Allison. "Ready?" He offered her his hand. "Hold on. We'll have to take the first several feet in darkness."

Allison clasped his hand. His grip was strong and sure. He dipped back into the cave, Allison right behind.

She was immediately overwhelmed by the complete

blackness inside the cave. The desert had been dark under the quarter moon, but nothing she had ever experienced compared to this. Not a sliver of starlight penetrated the solid walls of the cave.

The rock closed in around her. It was cool to the touch, not like the rock on the cliff face that still radiated the day's heat.

Terry pulled her gently through a tight bend. She was forced to twist her body to make the turn and suddenly felt an uncontrollable urge to scream, to turn and scurry from the cave. Claustrophobia wound tendrils of fear around her.

"Just another little bit," Terry was saying, still holding firmly to her hand.

Panic was building inside her. *Get a hold of yourself,* she commanded silently. *You've come this far; now finish the journey.* But the irrational fear swelled within her. She clamped her eyes closed and held her breath. Over and over she told herself, *I'm not going to scream.*

"This should be deep enough," Terry said. "The bend will block the light."

He switched on his flashlight, and Allison opened her eyes. The beam illuminated a chamber with sufficient height to stand in, though it was narrow and short. Just a few feet ahead it made a ninety-degree bend. The bright beam of the flash cast the walls in a white tone.

"Nervous?" he asked. He squeezed her hand reassuringly.

"A little," she answered truthfully. It was her first time in a cave, and she was surprised at the claustrophobia she had initially felt in the dark. The light helped to calm her somewhat, but the narrow walls served as a constant reminder that she was inside the earth. No matter how she tried, or perhaps because she was trying so hard, she could not rid herself completely of the image of the earth suddenly closing in on her.

"This has got to be the right cave," Terry was saying. "Everything matches the map. I wonder how Pedro Montoya ever found it."

Allison left him to mull the question silently as he guided her down the short walk to the bend. He turned the corner and shone his his flash into the next chamber. Allison stuck tightly behind him and peered over his shoulder. What she saw nearly made her faint.

A gleaming white skeleton lay propped against a wall of the cave. Remnants of tattered clothing still clung to the bones, and a pair of decayed boots remained on the feet.

Allison stared wide-eyed at the gruesome sight. Her arms involuntarily encircled Terry's chest.

He leaned forward, shining the flashlight fully onto the skeleton. "I'll be," he muttered under his breath.

Calm down, she told herself, relaxing her grip. A skeleton could cause no harm. Still, the sight of the brilliant white bones sent a shiver up her spine.

Terry stooped down to examine the skeleton. He played the light over the skull and down the tattered remnants of what had once been a shirt. Here and there ribs jutted from the ragged material.

"Look at this." He reached to the sandy floor alongside the skeleton, lifting a flat object, round and about the size of his palm.

"A belt buckle," he said, displaying it to Allison.

"Bronze, it looks like, and not too badly tarnished. The dry air in this cave preserved everything pretty well."

Initials had been molded onto the buckle. A large P and an M stood in raised relief.

"P.M.," Allison said. "Pedro Montoya."

"Must be," Terry answered quietly. "I guess we know what happened to him." On one knee beside the skeleton, he leaned his shoulder against the rifle, which he'd propped on the ground. "Look at this." He'd found a revolver.

She held the heavy weapon in her hands—Pedro Montoya's defense against those who would have stolen his gold. He had been wounded in a shoot-out in Agua Prieta, Mrs. Montoya had said, and, Allison surmised, he had returned here to reclaim his loot and leave. Only he had never left. He had died in the cave guarding his cache.

"I can't believe how well preserved that gun is," Terry said, balancing it in his hand. "It's a showpiece. Antique guns in this condition are worth a small fortune."

Allison gazed at Pedro Montoya's bones. She didn't feel that they had the right to disturb his final resting place. "Let's move on," she said.

Terry, noticing her distracted tone, clasped her hand and led her from the chamber.

Another twisting corridor followed. Allison negotiated the tight turns, feeling none of the panic that had initially gripped her. The cave, she realized, had existed for hundreds of years. She had nothing to fear from these cold stone walls.

They emerged into another chamber. This one was

larger than the previous two, with enough room to walk around in comfortably. It was also, apparently, the end of the cave, as no corridors led from it.

All these things Allison noticed only peripherally, for Terry's flashlight was shining directly on three wooden crates that had been stacked, one atop the other, against a wall at the far end of the chamber.

Terry bit his lower lip and glanced over his shoulder at Allison. She could see the excitement he was trying to conceal burning in his eyes. "The Confederate gold," he whispered.

"I don't believe it," Allison responded. She was breathless with anticipation.

The two of them stood for a moment, frozen at the entrance to the chamber, gazing at the wooden crates.

"Let's open them," Terry said at last, disturbing the deep silence of the cave.

He strode purposefully across the floor. Allison's heart pounded wildly in her chest as she followed. The palms of her hands were suddenly moist in the cool chamber. The legend *had* been real. They had discovered the lost Confederate gold.

Terry stood over the topmost crate, a screwdriver in his hand, while Allison shone the light. "Let's see what we've found," he said, poking the blade under a top plank.

The dry wood gave way easily. Terry worked quickly and methodically, prying around the edges of the crate, loosening all the nails.

At last all the planks that had once secured the top were ready to be removed.

"And now for the moment of truth," Terry announced, reaching across the crate and pulling the planking forward, exposing the contents inside.

Allison beamed the light into the crate. What she saw made her gasp.

Pinpoints of starlight dotted the sky. Allison could just discern the black outline of the cave entrance against the dark gray of the night. Ahead of her, Terry was shrugging his body through the opening.

Suddenly he stopped. "Shh," he hissed. His hand rested tensely on her shoulder. "Did you hear something?" he asked. He spoke in a voice so low that even in the stillness of the cave Allison could barely hear him.

"No," she answered, but her body was immediately rigid with concentration. Her ears strained for any sound. She heard a faint crunching.

"There," Terry said. "I heard it again." He pushed himself backward into the cave, pressing tightly against Allison. "Footsteps," he hissed, his breath warm in her ear. "On the ledge."

A cold chill ran up Allison's back. "Could it be an animal?" she asked, a thin vein of hope cutting through her fear.

Terry's shoulder dropped, and she heard him fumbling with his holster. "Don't know," he answered. He slid forward once again toward the cave entrance, gently allowing the rifle to rest on the cave floor. His body momentarily blotted out the starlight that seeped through the entrance; then Allison could see his silhouette framed against the night sky. The long, slender barrel of the revolver was even with his face and pointed upward.

Another rustling of stone on the ledge outside met Allison's ears.

Terry eased himself from the cave slowly. A small cascade of pebbles showered his back as he shimmied through the rift.

Allison held her breath. The noise sounded like an earthquake in the tomblike silence of the desert night.

Suddenly a white light shone on Terry's face. He twisted away, squinting against the beam, momentarily blinded by the dazzling glare.

Immediately a shot boomed, fracturing the calm. Terry's body jolted back against the cave entrance. The light went black, and a strangled scream filled the night, emanating from somewhere just outside the cave, growing faint, then abruptly ending.

"Terry!" Allison screamed. She pushed herself forward through the dark of the cave, oblivious to the scrapes and scratches being inflicted upon her by the narrow walls. "Terry!"

"I'm shot," he responded with a deep groan. He was lying half out of the cave, his torso resting on the ledge.

Allison grabbed him by the ankles, her only thought to prevent him from again being shot by pulling him back into the cave.

"No," he said, his voice sounding stronger. He pulled his legs up to his waist, then pushed himself forward onto the ledge. He pressed himself into a seated position with one arm and leaned heavily against the cliff face.

Allison scrambled onto the ledge beside him. Blood covered his shirtsleeve.

"I'll be all right," he said, his breath coming in heavy drafts. "Better than the guy who shot me, at least. He was standing on the narrow section of ledge when I popped my head out. He had a rifle. He must have lost his balance when he pulled the trigger."

That explained the sudden disappearance of the light and the scream she had heard. Allison sighed with relief. The Evil One was gone at last. Fate had finally finished his reign of terror.

She shone her flashlight on Terry's wound. The bullet had passed cleanly through the bicep. Blood seeped from small holes on both sides of his arm, but, she realized, the bone hadn't been broken. Just the same, his arm would be useless until he received proper medical treatment.

"This might hurt a bit," she told him, removing Terry's knife from the sheath on his belt and using it to cut open the front of his shirt. She peeled the material from his body and folded it into a bandage.

Holding the flashlight under her arm, she tied the makeshift dressing over the wound. He remained silent throughout the ordeal, though she was certain that he must be in considerable pain.

"That should help with the bleeding," she said, gently smoothing the bandage.

He grinned weakly. "Thanks." He closed his eyes and nodded. "It helps."

Suddenly a shot reverberated through the wash from the base of the cliff. Shards of rock exploded from the wall just over Allison's head. She ducked involuntarily.

"What's happening?" she asked. "Where did that come from?"

"The light," Terry shouted. "He sees the flashlight."

Allison snatched the light, still clamped under her arm, and switched it off. Another shot split the night. A bullet waffled the air over her head and ricocheted off the cliff with a screaming whine. "We've got to get back into the cave," she screamed.

Terry was using his good arm to push himself off the wall. Allison stooped over him and wrapped her arms around his chest. Using all her strength, she pulled him backward into the safety of the cave.

A third shot rang out from the wash. The bullet splattered into the rock beside the cave entrance. Allison stumbled backward over the rifle on the floor, falling almost flat on her back and breathing heavily from her exertion. Terry was on his side, his head resting on her knees. He moaned softly in pain.

"Are you all right?" she asked, sitting up, cradling his head in her hands. She kicked the rifle to the side.

"I'll live." He laughed weakly. "Be a little gentler. Keep in mind that I'm a wounded man."

Allison tried to catch her breath. "It must be the other brother down there shooting."

Her heavy breathing was the only sound inside the cave for several moments.

"You're right," Terry said, having recovered some strength. "No one could have survived a fall off that cliff. Both of the Ramirez brothers must have followed us here. One is out of the way, but the other is still armed, and he knows we're both in this cave."

"What do we do now?" she asked.

"I'm not going to be able to climb out. My arm would

throw me off balance, and I'd join our friend down there at the bottom of the cliff."

Allison considered Terry's wound and realized that there was only one answer to the predicament. They couldn't afford to simply wait for the situation to resolve itself. The killer in the wash would surely try to take the cave at daybreak, as soon as it was light enough to negotiate the trail. He wouldn't risk the same fate that had befallen his partner. And Terry was bleeding. Not heavily, but the constant seepage from the wound would surely weaken him. He needed medical attention as quickly as possible.

"I'll have to go alone," Allison decided.

Terry was silent for a moment. "I'm afraid so." He had evidently reached the same conclusion. "We have two guns. I'll give you the revolver. You can wear it in the holster. It won't slow you down at all."

"I don't know how to shoot," Allison said bluntly.

"I'll teach you right now." He hefted the pistol in his hand and passed it to her.

Allison held the weapon in her hands. It felt awkward and heavy. She doubted if she would ever be able to point it at a human being, much less pull the trigger. But, she realized, the revolver would be her only chance in the event of an encounter with the killer.

"Hold it in your right hand," Terry instructed. "Then cup your right hand into the palm of your left. You know how it's done—you've seen it in just about every cop-and-robbers movie ever made."

In the dark of the cave Allison followed Terry's instructions and lifted the gun to eye level, pointing it at the cliff wall, at the end of rigid arms in her best approximation of the police stances she had seen on TV. It was so dark in the cave that she could not even see the weapon in her hands, but she could feel its balance.

"If you have to shoot it," he said, "look down the barrel to be sure that you're pointing it directly at the target and pull the trigger. That's all there is to it. Hold it tightly, because it kicks and you don't want it flying out of your hands." He passed her the holster. "Buckle it on." Then after a moment of silence he added, "I hope you won't need it."

Allison adjusted the gun belt around her waist and wrapped the leg strap over her thigh. She slid the revolver into the holster.

"I'll be out on the ledge with the rifle," Terry said. "I'll be able to snipe at him. If he tries anything, I'll lay down some lead."

She was silent, contemplating the next few minutes, fighting the fear that welled within her.

"You're going to have to go *up* the trail," he told her.

"I know," she answered quietly. If she were to follow the trail down, she would simply end up in the wash with the killer. "I'll make the top of the mesa, then circle back to the trail we took on the way out here."

"Don't follow the exact route," he cautioned. "He may expect that."

"You'll need the water," she said, unstrapping her canteen.

"No. Take it."

Allison knew that with his steady blood loss, Terry would require all the water she could spare. "I'll pick up the supply we hid in the ravine," she told him.

"I don't want the water. Take it."

"It's time to go," Allison said, ignoring his remarks. Setting events into motion helped take her mind off the fear she was feeling.

Terry's arm was suddenly around Allison's shoulder. He was strong, confident. He pulled her close and kissed her tenderly on the lips. "You'll make it," he said.

Though she couldn't make out his face, Allison was certain that he was smiling at her. She kissed him softly. She wished she could be as certain of her success as he was.

"Let me set up on the ledge," he said, breaking the momentary spell. He pushed himself up and crawled slowly through the mouth of the cave, balancing on his two knees and his good hand. Upon reaching the ledge, he laid himself flat, pulled forward to the edge, and peered into the darkness of the wash below.

Allison, keeping low, pushed the rifle forward, and Terry aimed it into the darkness.

"One more thing," he whispered as she pressed herself to the cliff face and made ready to climb the trail to the summit of the cliff. "That pistol is a short-range weapon. If you suspect that you're being followed, hide yourself in some good cover and wait for whoever it is to show himself. Don't give in to fear and shoot wildly at targets that are out of range. You'll just waste ammunition and give away your position. Fifteen yards is about the limit of accurate shooting, I'd say."

"I hope I don't have to use it at all."

"Me too," he replied quietly.

She eased herself onto the ledge. Though the moon

was full, it had moved into the eastern sky, where it no longer provided direct illumination to the cliff face.

The deep shadow along the ledge would help to camouflage her from the killer, but the darkness also increased her chances for a misstep that could send her hurtling backward to the rocks below.

She pressed her weight against the cliff face and shuffled her feet slowly as the trail narrowed. The ledge was steep as well as narrow, and she knew it would take several minutes to traverse its length to the summit of the mesa. All the while, she knew, she would be exposed to the rifle of the killer.

She continued to inch up the ledge. Her arms were spread flat to the wall. Her cheek brushed the rock. Despite the cool of the desert night, she found herself perspiring heavily.

She fought the urge to rush her progress. The killer had obviously not yet realized that she was making her way up the face of the cliff. The only true danger lay in panic. *Slow down,* she commanded herself. A hurried step could be her last.

She could see the end of the trail drawing nearer through the gloom. The summit of the cliff etched a jagged line of black against the star-speckled sky.

The narrow ledge on which she was balanced began to climb steeply to the summit of the mesa. Her toes were jammed into the rock of the cliff, but the heels of her boots hung precipitously over the ledge. She moved lightly, slowly, methodically, on the balls of her feet.

Despite the danger of a fall Allison found herself growing calmer. The ledge was not posing as much of a threat as she had originally feared. Thank goodness, she thought, for her ballet training. She felt centered and in control on the narrow trail. She had only feet to go before she reached the summit.

She pushed forward and momentarily lost her balance. A section of the trail edge broke away and cascaded down to the wash below. To compensate for her lost balance, she pressed herself into the cliff face and clawed wildly for a handhold. Bits of gravel and stone streamed down the side of the mesa.

Within a second she had regained her balance. She held her breath and listened to the debris clattering down the cliff. In her heightened state of awareness, one hundred cannons firing in unison couldn't have made more noise.

She waited, not moving, poised on the strand of ledge, her heels hovering in space, her hands splayed across the rock.

"I'm all right," she hissed for Terry's benefit.

"Careful," she heard his muted reply.

Suddenly the night erupted in sound. Gunshots from the wash below boomed through the blackness. A bullet slammed into the cliff scant inches from Allison, splattering rock chips that caromed off her body. She began to scream with fear.

Immediately Terry opened fire from his protected position on the ledge. Small flames erupted from the barrel of the rifle with each shot.

"He's firing at the sound of the rocks you stumbled on," he shouted over the din. "It's too dark to see you."

Allison pressed her face into the hard rocks of the cliff and forced herself into silence. Screaming would just give away her position. It certainly wouldn't help matters. She bit her lip and held her breath. Standing on the ledge was beginning to take its toll. Her calf muscles ached from balancing on her toes.

Another fusillade of shots blasted from the wash. Allison turned her face in time to see Terry push himself back from the rim of the ledge. "He's firing at my barrel flash," he called. "Keep going."

For a moment she stood unmoving on the trail. Would Terry be able to fend off the killer while she ventured for help? She considered staying to help him fight but remembered his injury. Even as she waited, he was losing blood and strength.

She was his best chance for survival, she realized. She must escape to find help. Taking a deep breath, she resumed her steady shuffle toward the crest of the cliff as Terry unleashed another volley into the wash.

Night turned into day, and the blistering desert sun rose high into the sky. Insects burrowed into the cool of the earth, birds nested in the shelter of mesquite bushes, and lizards and snakes hid themselves in any shade they could find. Allison continued hiking through the rugged terrain.

Noon was fast approaching. Her lips were dry, and her throat was parched. Not far in the distance she could make out a depression in the desert floor that marked the entrance to the gorge where they had secreted their canteens.

She was breathing heavily, and perspiration soaked her shirt. Skirting the mesa had cost her valuable time, and hiking in the dark of night had further slowed her progress. After retrieving the canteens, she would have another four-mile hike to the Jeep, then the drive into Kingman.

She calculated how much time would be necessary to return with a rescue party for Terry and estimated that with the use of a helicopter they could return for him before sunset.

The thought of him wounded and trying to hold his position in the cave motivated her to step up her pace. An ugly thought crossed her mind, which she couldn't entirely block out. What if Terry had passed out from exhaustion and loss of blood? He would be defenseless. And, as Allison had already seen, the killers had never shown mercy to their victims.

She entered the declivity that led to the gorge and checked over her shoulder to mark her progress. The mesa was small in the distance. Rugged desert filled the gap.

Then she saw something that made her gasp in horror. A man suddenly emerged from a wash not half a mile distant. His face was blurred by the heat shimmers rising from the desert floor, but there was no mistaking the rifle in his hands. He was moving quickly, heading directly for Allison.

The killer. It had to be.

She turned quickly and forced herself to walk down the incline into the gorge. She didn't want to show her hand by running, thereby tipping the killer that she was aware of his presence. Not that he seemed to care. He had made no attempt to cover himself.

As soon as she was hidden inside the gorge, she began to run. For a crazed moment she considered the possibility that it was Terry whom she had seen, but she knew that his injury would have prevented him from hiking off the cliff.

A sickening thought clouded her mind. There was only one possible explanation. The killer had attacked the cave.

Hot tears of frustration and rage burned Allison's cheeks. That the killer was now on her trail proved what must have happened. Terry had passed out. The killer had murdered him in the cave, and now he was searching for Allison, the only living witness, not only to the crime but to the existence of the Confederate gold.

So many had died for the treasure. And now Terry was gone too. The thought drained her of strength, of her will to continue. She slowed her pace through the rocky corridor. The gorge was shrouded in shadow, and a cool breeze whispered through the cleft.

She wiped at her eyes. It was so unfair, she thought. She had never met a man like Terry. He had been so kind, so funny, so caring. She knew that she had loved him. That she had never told him so filled her with a sadness such as she had never known could exist.

She meandered disconsolately through the gorge. The killer was on her tail and closing rapidly, she knew. He was stalking her, like a cat stalks a mouse. She turned a bend and met a small, water-smoothed slab of stone that acted as a waterfall during rainstorms.

She remembered how difficult it had been to climb on the journey to the cave, not because of its height, which was no more than five feet, but because it had been worn nearly as smooth as glass by rushing water and sand.

She slid over the edge and landed in the sand flow at the bottom. The killer could make excellent time in the gorge, she knew. The traveling was all downhill.

The walls narrowed slightly after the waterfall and turned sharply. Allison made the bend, and an idea suddenly occurred to her.

Chapter Fifteen

*A*llison crouched in silence in the gorge, Terry's pistol in her hand. She remembered his advice. If she thought she was being followed, she should hide and let the fight come to her. Don't fire at a target more than fifteen yards away.

The distance would be no problem. The dry waterfall was barely ten feet distant, but she couldn't see it. She was hunkered down next to the wall of the gorge, just beyond the sharp bend.

She listened in silence, straining for any clue, any stray sound that might signal the approach of the killer.

It was the only way, she realized. Whoever was on her trail was a cold-blooded murderer. He was responsible for the deaths of Pancho and Esteban Montoya. And, she knew, he had also killed Terry. He wouldn't hesitate to kill her.

Her hopelessness and frustration had turned into something new. She forced herself to control her anger. The killer was brazen and bold. He thought he had nothing to fear from her. She eyed the revolver in her hands. He was wrong. She had only to wait for his arrival.

The sound of crunching gravel set her nerves tingling. She felt no fear. She knew what must be done. She had no choice, and this knowledge gave her strength.

The crunching on the gravel stopped. He must be at the top of the waterfall, she thought. It was almost time to make her move. She waited, tensed, every nerve in her body hot, every muscle coiled for the strike. There could be no mistakes.

Suddenly she heard it, the heavy thud as the killer leaped from the waterfall into the sand.

She sprang, turning the corner and leveling her gun on the murderer.

The killer held a rifle in one hand and was dusting his thighs with the other, unaware of Allison's presence.

"Drop the gun," she ordered.

He jerked his face toward her with surprise.

Allison felt a shock surge through her body. She was looking directly into the deep-brown eyes of Chief Perez.

A smile split his face, and he straightened, holding the rifle loosely by the barrel, the butt resting in the sand. "Forgive my surprise," he said softly. "But I was not expecting to meet you here."

"I'll bet you weren't," Allison said. The courage and anger she had been feeling while she crouched in waiting began to melt. Her adversary was no longer a nameless, faceless someone. He was a living human being. "Drop the gun," she ordered again.

"I think we can make a deal," Perez said.

"Drop it," she insisted. She was looking directly down the barrel of the revolver at his chest.

He didn't appear at all worried. "You don't know what you're doing," he said. "Put your gun down and we will deal."

The gun wavered in Allison's hands. She breathed heavily. Why wouldn't he drop his gun? The tension in the gorge was thick enough to cut. She continued to point the weapon, but her aim was skewed. "You killed Pancho," she stated, "and then you killed his father."

"Did I? You killed my deputy last night. Chuy Alvarez. He was a good man." His voice was strangely devoid of emotion. It had been Alvarez on the ledge.

Perez smiled wickedly. "The old man wouldn't cooperate. I tried to convince him that he should lead me to the gold, but he led me on a senseless hike through the desert instead. He wouldn't believe me when I told him the truth about his boy. He said he would never deal with his son's killer." Perez licked his lips. "He thirsted for revenge." His shoulders shook with high-pitched laughter.

Allison pictured Esteban Montoya dying of thirst in the desert, and suddenly it all became clear. He had tried to give a clue to the killer's identity. P . . . P . . . Perez!

"I tell you what," he said. "We can be partners."

Allison felt helpless. She held her gun on Chief Perez, but the weapon clearly did not intimidate him. The revolver alone was powerless to make him follow her commands. She blinked back tears of fear and frustration. The pistol wobbled in her hands.

His fingers inched down the barrel of his rifle. "I'll split the gold with you fifty-fifty."

The gold? Allison's heart leaped, but her gaze on Perez remained steady. It was possible that Terry was alive. Perez had obviously not entered the cave.

"Everyone will be happy," Perez continued. "We will both have what we want." He shrugged his shoulders innocently, as though he had just proposed a Sunday picnic in the park. His fingers continued inching down the barrel of the gun.

"Everyone will have what they want except Mrs. Montoya," Allison corrected him. She watched his hand continue its relentless crawl along the length of the barrel. "This is the last time I'm going to tell you. Drop it!"

"Are you to make me your prisoner?" he sneered. With the speed of a rattlesnake he whipped the rifle from the ground and propped the butt against his waist. He leaned back to steady the weapon, his finger already wrapping around the trigger.

The narrow gorge was filled with the deafening roar of a gunshot.

A look of shock and surprise crossed the chief's face. He smiled a wicked smile, dropped his rifle, and collapsed face forward in the sand.

Allison pressed back against the rock wall of the gorge, the pistol still held at the end of her extended arms. She hadn't fired the shot, but who had?

Her eyes darted along the walls of the ravine. Suddenly she spied someone along the top rim holding a rifle. She whipped her pistol around and leveled it on the figure.

It was a woman. Seeing the gun pointed at her, she dropped her weapon and raised her hands. "I mean you no harm," she called. "Now Pancho will be free."

It was Maria Diaz.

Chapter Sixteen

*I*n the end, Allison realized, it had been Pancho Montoya's inflated claims of great treasure that had fueled the entire affair.

A gentle breeze tousled her hair and carried on it the sweet scent of creosote. The nighttime sky was giving way to the fuzzy gray of early morning.

"Pancho started the ball rolling," Terry said. He placed his arm over her shoulders and pulled her close. His wound was healing well. "You remember how his mother said he liked to brag."

"We saw some of that ourselves," Allison reminded him, leaning into his strong body, recalling her first meeting with Pancho and Maria at the Montoya home one month earlier.

Pancho had been held captive in a tiny cell in the Nogales jail for over six months, but his incarceration hadn't dampened his obvious love for his fiancée. "She is the prettiest girl in Nogales," Pancho had said. "The most beautiful girl in all Mexico, in the entire world!"

Maria had held him as though she would never let him go, and the smiles and kisses had seemed unending.

"Esteban Montoya hadn't informed Pancho of the treasure, because he was afraid Pancho would tell," Terry said, "and sure enough, as soon as he learned of it, Pancho told the Ramirez brothers."

"But you can understand how that could happen," Allison countered. A cricket began chirping loudly nearby. "The Ramirez brothers had been threatening the Montoyas with the loss of their land. They wanted to build a new apartment building, and only the Montoyas stood in their way. They needed the Montoyas' land and were waiting for the lease to expire. They never dreamed that the Montoyas might actually have been able to buy the land."

Terry stared out at the desert. The morning sky was slowly brightening.

Pancho had become embroiled in an argument with Simon Ramirez and had angrily announced that his family would soon have enough money to own not only their land, but half of Nogales as well.

"The Ramirez brothers were worried," Terry said. "Their plans to build a new apartment would crumble if they couldn't grab the land the Montoyas were leasing."

The Ramirezes had turned to their friend Chief Perez to investigate Pancho's claims. They were no longer interested only in their apartment buildings, but in a possible treasure fortune as well.

The chief, however, had decided to cut the Ramirez brothers out of any future treasure find. He conducted his investigation quietly.

Perez and his deputy, Alvarez, had followed Pancho into the desert. They had captured him and interrogated him mercilessly, but Pancho had been unable to lead them to the treasure, because he hadn't realized that the map was drawn as a mirror image of the terrain.

"They didn't have the treasure," Terry continued, "but the chief could hardly turn Pancho free after kidnapping and torturing him."

The chief had become convinced that the treasure really existed, but he could not risk abducting the elder Montoya and creating two missing persons from the same family.

Instead, using threats to Pancho's life as coercion, he had enlisted the aid of Maria Diaz, Pancho's fiancée, to spy on her neighbors. Afraid of the consequences if she tried to defy Perez, Maria didn't dare tell the Montoyas that their son was still alive. If Esteban discovered the truth, he might do something rash that could get her beloved Pancho killed. When she learned that Esteban was ready to venture into the desert, she felt she had no choice but to inform Perez.

The chief and his deputy had trailed Esteban to the general location of the treasure, but Esteban had detected their presence. When he had tried to escape, Perez and his deputy had captured him. They'd offered him freedom in exchange for the treasure, but Esteban was convinced that Perez had killed his son and had refused to cooperate.

The chief and Alvarez had cut off Esteban's escape routes, hoping he would change his mind. But he hadn't, and the old man had wandered in circles until his death.

"He wouldn't believe that the chief had his son in

custody." Allison shook her head. "And he chose to die rather than deal with those he thought had killed Pancho."

"When we arrived to pay our respects to Mrs. Montoya, Maria noticed and followed us," Terry said. "It was her red car that kept popping up."

She had followed them as far as Tucson after their first visit to the Montoyas and had informed the chief of Allison's presence on the night of the kidnap attempt.

Perez and his deputy had set the ambush and would probably have kidnapped and tortured Allison if not for the miraculous intervention of the stranger.

Allison ran her fingers over her throat and shuddered, recalling the awful events of that night. "I was lucky."

Terry tightened his grip around her shoulders. "Maria knew that Pancho would be held until the treasure was found," he said, "so she cooperated with Perez. But when Esteban was murdered in the desert, she realized what ruthless men she was dealing with and devised her own plan to set Pancho free."

Allison had witnessed the result. Maria had trailed Perez and Alvarez into the desert as they followed Terry and Allison. On the night of the shoot-out at the cave, she had crept close enough to the chief's camp to hear the deputy's fall and the ensuing firefight. When she had realized that the chief was setting off from his position, she had scavenged for the deputy's rifle and had followed.

"Perez heard me trip on the ledge and realized that I was trying to escape," Allison said. "He must have guessed that you were wounded because you were stay-

ing. He headed back in the direction from which we'd
come, hoping to intercept me. He probably spotted me
in the morning and finally closed the gap between us
in the gorge."

But he hadn't noticed Maria following him, and during his showdown with Allison he had paid for his inat-
tention.

The two women had made Kingman, and a rescue
copter had been dispatched. Terry had been found in
good condition and had required only a short stay in
the hospital. For Perez and his deputy, rescue was su-
perfluous.

Terry and Allison were silent. They were standing
atop the sand dune they had climbed that first day,
when they had discovered Esteban Montoya dying in
the nearby wash.

A slight morning breeze was rolling across the desert,
pushing away the darkness. They had left in the middle
of the night to return here one last time, to view the
sunrise from this never-to-be-forgotten place.

So much had happened in these past two months, Allison thought. The deaths of Esteban Montoya and
Chief Perez, and the hunt for the Confederate gold.

She smiled ruefully. The legend of the lost treasure
had been nothing more than that—a legend. The
stacked crates in the cave had contained not gold, but
weapons. Rifles to aid the Confederate rebels in Arizona.

The antique arms had been well preserved in the desert climate, however, and had commanded quite a sum
when sold at auction.

"I imagine that Pancho Montoya inherited his braggadocio from his ancestors," Terry said. "Pedro Montoya probably intercepted some guns but made it sound as if he'd looted the Spanish Armada."

"Well, that's what legends are made of." Allison laughed.

She and Terry had given all the money to Mrs. Montoya, who was in the process of rebuilding her home and adding a guest house, on the same plot of land she had leased for so many years. She had finally purchased the land from the Ramirez brothers, who, it turned out, had been innocent of any wrongdoing in the entire affair. Pancho and Maria were to be married when the guest house was completed.

Terry's arm tightened on Allison's shoulders. She put her arm around his waist. "It won't be long, now," Terry said. The first faint rings of color were rising on the horizon.

Allison pressed her cheek into Terry's chest. She felt safe here with him, and secure. Her memory flashed for an instant to the leering face of Chief Perez. She blinked her eyes, trying to wipe his face from her mind.

"I've almost finished my book," she mentioned, chasing the unpleasant memories away. She had been keeping secret the progress of her literary endeavor.

"Really?"

She stood back with a smile. "You don't need to sound so surprised."

Terry chuckled. "I knew you would do it. What's it about?"

"Guess," she teased.

"Could you narrow it down some?"

"Well. . . ." Allison hesitated. "I suppose so." She

eyed Terry with a smile. "It's about a man and a woman—"

"Sounds good so far."

"Who go searching for gold in the desert."

Terry smiled. "Seems I've heard this somewhere before. How does it end?"

"I said *almost* finished. The ending isn't written yet."

"There are all sorts of possibilities."

Allison watched him thoughtfully.

"Do you intend to let me read this book of yours someday?" Terry asked.

"Maybe."

"How long before it makes the best-seller list?"

Allison laughed. "We might wait forever on that. I'd be happy just to see it end up on a library shelf somewhere."

Terry nodded. His hands were on her waist. "What's the title?"

Allison stared up at the sky and pretended to think. Only a few stars were visible in the purpling heavens. "How does *Desert Gold, Desert Fear* sound?"

Terry shrugged. "Well, we certainly found fear," he said noncommittally.

"A title can always be changed," she told him, noting his indifference. "Anyway, we never did find any gold."

"Maybe we did." His arms circled around her, and he pulled her close. He kissed her lightly.

She slid her arms around his neck and gazed into his eyes.

"I love you," he said softly.

Allison thought she would melt in his arms. "I love you too." Her hands stroked the backs of his shoulders.

He was so strong, so sincere. She had nothing to fear from him.

He smiled and again kissed her softly. "You say your book isn't finished?"

"Almost."

"I have a perfect ending," he said. "One sentence. Would you like to hear it?"

She tilted her head. "I think so."

He leaned forward and whispered in her ear. His warm breath sent ripples of pleasure up her spine. Then he was embracing her, holding her tightly and kissing her as only a man in love is capable of kissing.

Allison wrapped her arms around him and returned his kisses.

The first orange rays of sunlight lit a new desert day as his words echoed joyfully in her mind.

Their future together had just begun.